SUN SPOT MAGIC

BONNIE ELIZABETH

My Big Fat Orange Cat Publishing

Sun Spot Magic
My Big Fat Orange Cat
Middle Grade Fantasy December 2017

Copyright 2017
Bonnie Elizabeth Koenig

Cover Image Copyright © Syda_Productions | Deposit Photo
Cover Copyright Bonnie Koenig

My Big Fat Orange Cat Publishing
MyBigFatOrangeCat.com

For the readers who love Willow Vaughn

Chapter One

There are certain wishes the power won't grant — *The Fairy Godmother Handbook*

All I really wanted this summer was to find a job and get a car. I had just turned sixteen and I was ready to make my own decisions and go where I wanted without having to ask my parents to drive me.

You'd think that being a fairy godmother would mean I could just wish a car into being, but that's not how things work, because, rules. I have to live at home and I have to do things the ordinary way because I'm underage. Blah, blah, blah. That's right. I'm Willow Vaughn and I'm a fairy godmother. It's weird, I know, but I'll get to that.

I'd started putting in job applications and was waiting by the phone to hear from managers. I thought the hardest part would be getting an interview, because let's face it, I'm only sixteen, so it's not like I have any work experience and there were a lot of people like me. Some of them older, and, according to my dad, more reliable. My dad talks about reliability because he worries that I might not be very good at showing up when I say I will.

I was out to prove him wrong by getting that job and showing up for work when I needed to and then saving for my car. Except the sun spots happened.

Apparently sun spots and magic don't mix well, which means that all fairy godmothers were going to have problems. It wasn't something I knew about before because I'm new at this whole fairy godmother thing. It's not like I'd been doing it for very long. I still remembered how it all started in vivid detail.

I'd made a wish that could be interpreted that I wanted to be a fairy godmother, so *bam*. Here I am, granting wishes, about one a week or so. So I'm not like a real fairy or anything. I'm one hundred percent red-blooded, grass-fed, locally grown, organic teenager. Like most people my age, I'm a little snarky and have a reputation to uphold. Of course, granting wishes has mitigated some of my issues, but still, I *am* only sixteen and that's a tough age, according to my mom.

Part of being a fairy godmother means having to attend these godawful meetings on Monday at seven p.m. sharp, every single week for the rest of my life, which could be like really, really long if I decide to remain a godmother because, like, we don't age, or age only a little, or something like that. It's one of the perks of getting the wish-granting power bestowed on us.

So one Monday night in June, there I was, trying to sink as far into the old, brown, fugly as crap sofa that we had in the basement where we meet. My feet were chilled but not completely freezing. After my first time at the meetings, I knew to wear my shearling boots, because this is like the skankiest place ever. It's an old basement with concrete walls and water that drips from a pipe in the corner. The furniture is lumpy and the sofa could swallow you whole if you weren't careful, but on one end it's probably the best seat in the house, and believe me, when I arrive, I make a beeline for it every single time. Yeah, it smells a little like wet dog, but what can you do?

So it's a mixed bag. At least it's Monday night and not, like, Friday or Saturday, because I'd have had to bow out right away, except you can't. The only way to get out of being a fairy godmother is to grant someone else's wish to help other people. The real hardcore folks who want to help aren't exactly out there saying "I wish." They're in 'the trenches', as my mother would say.

There are only about ten of us here. I've learned over the seven or eight months of being a fairy godmother that our group isn't the only one. And powers grow with seniority. I know all of that because I screwed up on a wish big time a few months ago.

One of the things we do at these meetings is check in, kind of see how the week went with wish granting. If there were problems, we all got to discuss them. Sometimes we even learned something, although that didn't happen much, because apparently the full-blooded fairy godmothers—yes there are those, too—don't usually bother to do any teaching. They just complain a lot.

Tonight it was Grace's turn to be on the hot seat. I've been there, believe me, and it was the worst. I granted this wish that took me to this alternate world where everyone was horrible, I mean, like, *really* horrible, and not just horrible in the way that they are every day. I get an icky feeling even remembering it.

This time Grace had messed up.

Grace is one of the people who were older when they became fairy godmothers, so I tend to think of her as Granny. She wears old lady dresses that are practically see-through, like she can't afford real clothing or something. You'd think someone would have helped her get a wish for money, but no, that's what she wears. You can see her bra through the dress, and it always bothers me. I like Grace but it'd be nice if she'd learn to dress herself in something that wasn't tissue thin, you know?

Anyway, she was talking about her experience, kinda slow, the way old folks talk, and I was sitting there, just glad it wasn't me this time.

"She said she wished to have him back. It's not normally the sort of wish we can grant—I mean her husband was dead—and when she'd made her wish, I wasn't paying attention, really. I was looking for someone to help with a wish, but I felt my power go out to her like it would have if I had let it go, and suddenly she's holding this corpse. He was still dead and decaying—he'd been dead about a month…" Grace trailed off.

"And I did that. But we can't do things like that!" Grace blew her nose into a tissue. She'd been using several of them.

Grace, I'm pretty sure is American, or maybe Canadian. I know Paula, one of the other fairy godmothers, is in the United States because I found her on Facebook. We've even become friends on it, even if we don't have much in common.

Grace isn't on social media as far as I can tell. I haven't gone looking for anyone else. I mean, one guy's name is Jesus, and how would that look if I friended Jesus? That's all I know about him,—like he doesn't even have a last name. And no, he doesn't say it like 'Jesus.' He says it the Spanish way, so maybe he's from Mexico or South America. Jesus doesn't say much.

There's this big guy Brian, who looks like a football player, but he just laughs about American football and talks about soccer, so I'm pretty sure he's not from here either. And Sergei, well, bad Russian spy movies come to mind. He even has a Russian accent—like, can you believe it?

"I got a message the other day," Paula said, when Grace paused to sniff. "From that woman, Brin?"

I perked up and Paula nodded at me.

Deliza even looked interested from where she sat in her favorite spot, the ugly, gray chair, which was one of the most uncomfortable places as far as I was concerned, but Deliza was really tall so maybe it worked for her. She always huddled like she was trying to make herself smaller and was the quietest person I have ever met. Maybe it's because she's the only black woman there and she doesn't feel welcome, but I have a feeling she's just shy.

"It's part of Brin's movement to keep us more educated about what we're doing," Paula said, continuing with her story. It would probably take some time to get to, because Paula was going to have to explain everything, in case someone did the impossible and missed a meeting.

Also, 'a movement' was probably an overstatement. It was more like a general suggestion than a movement.

"Anyway, Brin sent an email that said there are particularly active sun spots going on, which is going to cause problems with our wish granting. If you have to grant a wish in the next two weeks, be careful and try to do it during the evening hours. It's less likely to get interfered with."

"I guess if it's dark, we aren't facing the sun, so whatever the sun spots are doing to interfere shouldn't be as strong during the night hours," Sergei said. I always feel weird when he talks and I have to think about his name.

I mean Bob would be so much more normal. Russian spies are not named Bob, so I wouldn't feel like I was in a really bad old spy movie whenever he talked. Or maybe I would, just with a Russian spy named Bob, which would probably mean it was a comedy movie rather than a bad thriller.

"Anyway," Paula went on, "It appears that this activity is going to last about two weeks, which means for most of us there are two wishes that could go wrong. We should all practice our meditations."

After my disastrous wish, I had learned from Brin that you can make sure you don't hear certain wishes if you have a meditation of some sort. So now we had to practice and talk about our practice. With the sun spots, chances were we'd be talking a whole heck of a lot about our meditations.

That *so* did not excite me. But let's get real. What about meeting in a basement with a bunch of people all way older than I was *was* exciting? Um yeah. Nothing.

I counted back to when I had last granted a wish. I was coming close to being due. My luck? I'd be one of those who got to grant three wishes when there were sun spots. Great. Just what I needed, more wish mess-ups. Because, here's the thing. I didn't know there were non-human fairy godmothers before I'd messed up a wish. I just thought we were all, like, the same—humans who had wished and gotten this power.

It's not like that. There are what they call full-blooded fairy godmothers, and if you think that old men granting wishes to little girls is creepy, well, the full-blooded one I met was kind of worse. Because he seemed like he might be a cop in a cop show, but he had a certain sleaziness that I couldn't ever put my finger on. And Brin, who was there, said a few things that made think it wasn't all that innocent on his part. So. Yeah. No bad wishes for me.

I *so* did not want to be noticed.

"What did you do?" Connie asked Grace. "I mean, if a wish goes wrong, what do we do?"

"I think our warning was that we should try and not make those bad wishes, but if we need help cleaning it up, then we call a senior," Paula said.

Grace nodded. "Fortunately, while the woman was completely undone, there were other people around and they gathered up the body. It made the news and everything but then it calmed down. I was so shocked I didn't even think about calling for help to have it reversed. And really, the damage was already done. So far as I know, we can't turn back time."

I didn't suggest that the full-bloods probably could. They seemed pretty darned powerful if they cared to use their powers.

I tried not to sigh or fidget. This sofa was comfortable for a short time, but fidget too much and you start sinking down into the depths, and then you'll have your butt stuck there for the rest of eternity unless someone helps you out.

Cole mumbled about something. Sue glared at him.

On his side of the room, Sergei nodded quietly, thinking. Paula tried to get us all to do some meditation but fortunately this group of old folks had as much interest as I did in group meditation. Finally we were done discussing and I could leave.

Thank heavens. I was more than a little ready to get out of that room. And hopefully not have to grant any wishes. Of course, I did know about the meditation and hopefully I could hold off a wish pressure until after dark. I drew in a breath as the room faded, hoping that things would go okay.

Naturally they didn't.

Chapter Two

Underage Fairy Godmothers, as defined by the cultural standards of the day, will abide by additional rules — From the Fairy Godmother's Handbook

I woke up Tuesday morning feeling vaguely like I might have a wish building. It was just my luck, on the first day of the sun spots, when we are supposed to be being careful and trying not to grant wishes during daylight, that I woke up with wish pressure. It was so unfair. I mean, come on. First thing in the morning? Even a small wish was likely to get uncomfortable before evening.

I kicked off my lavender comforter, smelling the faint traces of coffee from downstairs, and got up, late-ish, but not super late. My mom doesn't go in for that. In fact, the amount of noise she was making, walking around like she weighed fifteen hundred pounds, so that I could hear her even if she was downstairs, meant she was hoping to wake me up. While I don't have a job, yet, I don't get to totally sleep in.

Of course, I wanted a job. My deal with my dad was

that if I could earn and save a thousand dollars, he would match it, and I could get my own car. That was my goal for the summer. Find some place to work part time and maybe by the end of summer, I'd have a car. I could still work to save up for other stuff I wanted, like, say a better computer, more music, and important things like that, because Dad was going to pay the car insurance.

I heard my brother, Eric, open the door to the bathroom we share, so he was probably working today. Eric just started junior college. He wanted to go to a four-year, but the costs were too high, and my mom was all worried about student debt. I mean normal parents would have just worried about money but my mom was worried about what that kind of debt would do to his health.

So Eric's still at home, going to classes. He's taking one course this summer so he can have a lighter load in the fall. He got a job shortly before he graduated, at one of those big, warehouse, home improvement places. He's stuck in plumbing, which means he has all sorts of really gross toilet stories to tell.

Now, I want a job, but I totally don't think I could do that. I mean, I know nothing about fixing things around the house, except if the toilet runs too long you jiggle the handle, and when the air conditioning fan starts making a squeal, I have to run outside and slam my fist against the outside of it just a hand span from the top to make it stop. My dad taught me that one. My mom can't seem to get it right, but I can. Every. Single. Time. #teenwin.

Unfortunately there's not much call for that kind of thing as far as paying jobs go.

I pulled a pair of gray shorts and a pink tank top with a built-in shelf bra out of my pale, maple wood dresser—which my mom refused to replace—and put them on. I glanced around my room. It was kind of messy, but then it always is. The lavender and black stripes my mom and I had painted on the walls looked a bit oppressive until I opened the blinds. Then I went downstairs.

In the kitchen, I grabbed some yogurt and berries from the large stainless steel fridge that could have housed a small family. I used one of the pottery store bowls—locally made, of course, because, my mom—to mix everything, tossing in a handful of walnuts from the dark wood cabinets that I had a feeling my mom would hate in another few years and insist upon changing. I kind of hated them now. They looked like they belonged in an old haunted house movie or something.

When I was little, we had white cabinets that didn't catch smudges. Then we had this light wood, sort of maple color, and now we have a coffee black color. The counter used to be granite, but now it's some sort of natural concrete that isn't so porous. Mom swears she's not going to change the kitchen again. I wouldn't count on it. She loves being there too much not to change it often. Even if her constant updating and remodeling isn't totally environmentally sound.

I sat at our old, round, pine kitchen table. We have a bigger table in the dining room that mom usually has set with placemats and a vase. Now and then she even remembers flowers. Mostly, though, we eat in the kitchen despite having a dining room. I looked out the window at the yard. The sun was already moving across the grass making everything bright and hot-looking. The *click click* of the air conditioner kicking in told me I was right about the whole hot thing.

I had been thinking of going to the mall with Sage, but if it was going to be that hot, I wasn't that excited. I wanted to pick up store applications, and I didn't think I should just wear shorts for that. Which meant I'd be overdressed for outside and there are places to wander around outside, too.

While I munched the berries in my yogurt, I decided I'd go online and see who had applications on their websites, and try that first. Then, when I texted with Sage later on, I could probably feel okay about just going to the mall in shorts.

My mom isn't very enthusiastic about me getting a job. She'd probably recommend I go to the pool, which was certainly an option. Maybe Sage would prefer to do that. We hadn't been there in, like, a week.

I considered texting her now, but Sage wasn't likely to be up before ten. Her mom worked, which meant she got to sleep in until she wanted to get up. Actually, sometimes her mom made her get up before she left for work, but then she got to go back to bed if she wanted. I mean, what was her mom going to do? Call her every five minutes?

"Don't even think of telling her that," Sage once told me. "She'd probably do it."

Yeah, her mom probably would. I'm surprised she didn't pay my mom to go across the street to make sure her daughter was up and about at a decent hour. What is it about moms?

By the time I finished my breakfast and was putting the spoon and bowl in the dank hole that's our black, steel sink, the wish pressure had grown. A lot. Which sucked because it wasn't even ten on the first day of sunspots, and I was going to have to grant a wish.

I went back up to my room. My mom would see the dish and spoon in the sink and know I was up. That way she wouldn't worry that I was upstairs dying. And yes, that's so totally my mom.

I laid across my bed, which, naturally I hadn't made, so it was nice and lumpy with covers pushed here and there, and pulled out my MP3 player and earbuds and turned up the music really loud. I had learned that if I breathed in and out and listened to music, I wouldn't hear any wishes, at least not until the wish pressure got really, really strong. I hoped that it would help as this wish need built. If I couldn't hear a wish, I couldn't grant it, right?

Seemed like a plan. And for a while it seemed to be working. The pressure built and sometimes I'd look down expecting to see my stomach had risen up and was huge, about to burst, like a pregnant woman about to have a baby, but no such thing. I looked all normal.

But the wish pressure was getting stronger—strong enough that even with the music I was listening for someone to say "I wish."

I changed my music to something faster and wilder, a constant beat. I couldn't do anything too slow and dreamy, it pulled me out. The beat was my lifeline to avoid granting a wish. I had no idea how well that would work, because I'd never had to avoid granting any wish before. I'd only ever had to try and avoid listening to one wish, not all of them.

Then my mom came in. Right. I know. She might have knocked, but there was no way I'd hear her.

"Willow?" I could just make out her voice.

I waved, opening my eyes.

"For God's sake. Why don't you get up and go out and do something? It's after ten. Sage is probably even up by now."

I just smiled. "I am doing something." I mean, I was. I was listening to music and trying to avoid granting a wish during the daylight hours.

My mom shook her head.

"You need to get out and get some sun. I wish you'd make more use of that pool this summer."

And with that, the wish flowed out of me.

I saw the pink cloud that always flowed when I granted wish. Sometimes I guided it, but this time it swirled between me and my mom like a cotton candy bomb had fallen. My mom had a laundry basket and was picking up the pile of clothing near my desk. She didn't seem to notice the cloud.

The effects of that wish hit me right away. I got the sudden urge to leap off the bed and go throw myself into the pool. In fact, it took a heck of a lot of willpower not to just go running outside and dive in.

Great. I was the subject of a wish I had granted. This was *so* not supposed to happen. I mean, not just that it was annoying and did happen, but I wasn't supposed to be able to grant wishes about myself.

I quickly pulled on my swimsuit, made sure I had my phone, my music, and my towel, which was in a bag near the door of my room from the last time I'd gone to the pool. I was out the door wearing only my flip flops, and running off, yes, *running*, before my mom got back downstairs from tossing in a load of laundry.

Chapter Three

---

*Fairy godmothers can't grant their own wishes — The Fairy
Godmother Handbook*

The pool sits smack-dab in the middle of the
subdivision, about seven or eight blocks from our
house, depending on how you count that long stretch that
curves by some trees. Supposedly that space was to
increase housing values, or so Lauren's mom said. All I can
say, is who would want to live by the treed area? That's
where all the crazy axe murders hang out.

At least the shade cooled me down, and the trees
smelled better than the garbage someone had put out a
day early.

Fortunately, I didn't manage to trip myself up with the
flip flops, because let's just say running in them isn't easy.
Still, I had to concentrate way more on my running than I
should have, and I could only imagine my mother shaking
her head if she saw me racing to the pool.

The pool requires an ID to get in. Fortunately I had
one of those with me. I worried when I got there, breath-

less, sounding like I was about to have an asthma attack, that I'd forgotten it. It's not that I'm out of shape, but running in flip flops is really hard. Did I say that already?

It took me only a minute of searching through the tote I'd grabbed to find it. The lifeguard on duty, a skinny dark-haired guy, let me into the pool area, through the archway that had a women's room on one side and a men's room on the other. It also had the "mechanical room"—I have no idea what that is—and then an office area for the lifeguards to sit in and cool off when they got too hot.

I was glad I ate breakfast, because I had a feeling Mom's wish was going to make me feel guilty for leaving the pool area to eat some lunch. I knew I could probably leave and come back, but then I'd lose the good lounger I was going to grab. If I had to stay out by the pool, I wanted a good place to sit.

It was only a little after ten, so there were just a few moms with small kids around. I quickly found one of the white loungers that was in the sun now and would be shaded by the eves of the building when the afternoon rolled around. Normally I like the sun, but I didn't want to get too much.

My pre-packed tote bag saved me again by having my sun screen in it, so I wouldn't completely fry. I wondered what my mom was thinking.

Next Monday, I was so going to have to ask how I had been able to grant a wish that affected me. And if there was a way to undo it. I mean, I *so* didn't want to be at the mercy of the pool all summer. This was, like, *so* not good. How was I going to go to work if I had to hang out at the pool?

I lathered up with sun screen and then dove into the water. It wasn't that cool, because we'd had temps in the high nineties for days. Still, I was there, fulfilling my mother's wish. I did ten laps of crawl stroke before I felt like I had worked off some of the anxiety that had been building while I sat next to the pool putting on sun screen.

This was going to be bad. Mom's wish had been that I make more use of the pool. Apparently, the wish decided that for the pool to be 'of use,' meant I should be in it. The good news, as I splashed around, and while my breathing calmed down, was that last year I had only gone to the pool about twice a week for maybe two hours a day. I'd only spent maybe a half an hour swimming each time.

Hopefully, that would work out to me spending maybe an hour in the pool and a couple of hours on the lounger. Hopefully. You never knew.

I *so* shouldn't have been able to grant that wish. I've read the manual, because, like, even though it's beyond boring, there were things I needed to know. And it says in there very clearly that you can't grant a wish about yourself. Something was wrong.

If that could go wrong, what if I didn't just have to spend a few hours a week at the pool? What if I, like, had to *live* there or something? This would so not be good for getting a job, plus it would make my dad mad, because we'd talked about how getting a job was a responsibility and this would totally seem irresponsible to him. Considering he already thought I was a little bit irresponsible, well, being stuck at the pool all the time could be the worst.

I completely wanted to prove my dad wrong on the responsibility thing. He'd been real excited about helping me consider options for work. I mean, if I couldn't get a job because of the pool wish, I'd be completely disappointed and stuck at home because I didn't have a car. My dad would be "disappointed" because I'd let him down.

He was the one who told me to apply at the grocery store because I'd get paid better there than if I worked at a dress shop. Not to mention, it would be way closer to home. There were three grocery stores close by, and I had put in applications at all of them last Friday. I was waiting to hear. If I was stuck at the pool, I could only hope that I could force myself to go to an interview if I got one.

There was so much wrong with this wish I could not even… I sighed. I drew a breath to dive to the bottom and swim along its length as far as I could.

Coming up, I wiped my hands over my face. I did that a few more times. Then I just spent some time bouncing around the deep end, not doing much. I laid on my back and floated. If only I had one of those inflatable rafts. I wondered what my mom would do if I asked her for one.

I got out of the water and flopped down on the lounger and picked up my phone. There was a text from Sage asking me where I was.

I texted back that my mom was being annoying and I'd gone to the pool to get away from her. There. That would hold Sage. Too bad she hadn't been around so Mom could have wished this on both of us. Then I wouldn't have to keep making excuses about why I wanted to be at the pool.

This could be a very long summer.

A moment later Sage told me she was on the way. Great. I could get back in the pool. And I wanted to. With my luck, my mother's wish was going to turn me into a prune.

Chapter Four

If someone wishes for you to change your behavior, you cannot grant that wish — The Fairy Godmother Handbook

Sage and I stayed at the pool until close to three. We left because we were both hungry. After swimming and horsing around in the pool when she first got there, we lathered up the sun screen—me for the second time, her for the first. We laid out on the loungers, chatting, listening to music, and texting back and forth and with our friends, Lauren and Ashley.

Sage was getting hungry by late afternoon so I called my mom to come pick us up. She was not pleased with me running out.

"Just because I said spend more time at the pool, doesn't mean I wanted you to go running out right that second. You could have waited. Said good bye," she said when I walked out the fancy black iron gate to the parking area. "And you should have taken some water. What did you do? Drink from that drinking fountain?"

I could see her getting ready to talk about germs, even

though, yes, I had taken drinks from that fountain. I was thirsty and had no desire to leave the pool thanks to her. But I wasn't going to admit it.

"It just sounded really good," I said. "And I wanted to be sure to get a good spot that would be in the shade this afternoon."

It was a good story. I mean there were people vulturing around, waiting for when Sage and I left our loungers, practically scrambling to grab them before our stuff was even moved. People can be so rude.

My mom just gave me a suspicious look, but didn't say anything. Fortunately, no one other than Sage was there, so she couldn't grill anyone else about my eating and drinking habits.

Back at my house, Sage and I said our goodbyes and she headed off for her house. I went inside to shower and cool off. Even in the shade, it was hot out.

While Sage had been hungry, I'd gotten warm enough that I didn't have much of an appetite, but still, I ate something to appease my mom. She made me a sandwich with homemade bread (always at our house) and special, angel-blessed deli meats that she gets from one of the organic grocers around here, plenty of grass-fed butter, and home-made mustard and other crap like that. It was pretty good.

Mom had not been pleased that I hadn't applied to any of the organic grocers. They were a pretty long way away, so I'd have had to arrange to borrow the car or get a ride and that would have been a hassle. I could walk to two of the normal grocers, although one was a hike, and my dad drove by the other one back and forth to work, so he said he'd make sure I always had a ride.

Which was way easier than trying to negotiate with my mom who wasn't at all excited about the idea of me working so I could have my own car. Up until he started working this summer, my brother had always just borrowed Mom's car, but she was always way easier on him. If I tried that, and I had once or twice, she was always grilling me about where I was going and when I'd be back and letting me know that she expected me to let her know if I stopped anywhere else, even when it was on the way home because, you know, someone might murder me to get her old Prius, because *that* happens. Apparently my brother was expected to fight off these killers-in-waiting.

After eating, I went back to my room and decided to look through the fairy godmother handbook just to look up things like granting wishes against ourselves. As I thought, we didn't normally have the power to grant a wish that would affect us directly. I mean, many times wishes had an effect on our lives if we knew the person wishing. But normally I shouldn't have been able to grant a wish that would change my behavior.

I made a mental note to let the others know what had happened. Maybe someone would have a need to grant a wish and then I could un-wish the pool thing or something. Usually that didn't work but with the sun spots maybe it would.

Unfortunately, it would be a week before I could even ask. Until then, unless I wanted to try and get someone to help me call on one of the seniors, it looked like I was stuck going to the stupid pool. I sighed. This was going to be a very long two weeks, and probably an even longer summer.

My phone started jingling with texts. First it was Sage telling me that she'd gotten a nasty burn despite all the sun screen.

I looked at my skin. It was turning a bit pink but I was pretty good. I was lucky. I didn't burn that easily.

I texted back.

Then I got something from Lauren asking if I wanted

to go to a movie that evening. I said I would love it. Sage was already on the text and she was going, too.

I went down and told my mom about the invitation. Seeing there wasn't any school, I doubted she'd have a problem.

"What time?" she asked.

"They're going to the five o'clock show, and then we were going to grab a bite after." This would be her sticking point. Food. She hated it when I didn't eat food at home. My mom has this paranoia that I'll eat something and turn up dead because it wasn't organic and local and grass-fed. I never tell her about the soda I drink when I'm out.

"You ate out once this week already…" she was shaking her head.

"But you just made me this huge sandwich, so I probably won't want much. It'll be late. Probably just a snack." I tried to look wide-eyed and innocent, which isn't something I do easily.

My mom gave me a long look before shaking her head. Finally she said okay.

I raced back up the stairs and flopped on my bed, texting even before I hit the bed covers.

"I'm in," I said. "Mom said it was fine."

"Pick you up soon," Lauren texted back.

At least I wouldn't have to worry about granting wishes and sun spots for a few hours. For a few, I could go back to my normal, teenaged girl routine. Which is important. Little did I know that that would be one of the best times I was going to have for the next couple of weeks.

Chapter Five

Rarely will there be enough sun spot activity to interfere in the wish-granting process — from a future Fairy Godmother's Handbook

Of course things couldn't be that easy. Yeah, the movie was good. Yeah, we ate good food and I had a burger and fries, which is my go-to out-of the-house food. And I had a soda. I'm a huge fan of Dr. Pepper. I'm sure I like it because it's the sweetest of the sweet and I just don't get enough of that in my house. My mom would be completely horrified.

I have decided that when I'm an adult, I am *so* going to live on junk food.

At any rate, the evening was good. The next day, less so.

I woke up to hear my mother humming to herself outside my room. It was just past seven, not even my usual wake up time. I must not have slept well. I felt a wish pressure. At first I thought it might be gas, because of all the good food but then I realized that didn't feel right.

Instead, I had another wish building. What was up with

that? I mean, yeah, wishes don't come in nice, predictable intervals, but, at least for me, they had never come this close together. Just my luck to have that happen when there were sun spots. Plus, it was first thing in the morning, *again*. This was *so* beyond irritating.

Like I was going to have to try and hold this in for the day again. Look what happened yesterday.

I got up, even if it was a little early, and dressed in my jean shorts and a tank. This time I put my bikini on underneath because I was already thinking I wanted to be at the pool. Then I combed through my hair, pulling it all back in a ponytail, which left my pink highlights like a long streak down one side.

Downstairs, Eric was still at the kitchen table, spooning oatmeal into his mouth. He had a book that looked like it weighed as much as I do sitting in front of him. He put down his spoon to turn a page. Instead of picking it back up, he grabbed bacon from a plate. My mom clearly thought he deserved to have a good breakfast. She never makes breakfast for me.

"Don't you rate," I said.

"Morning to you, too, sunshine," Eric said, not looking at me.

I pulled out my usual yogurt and fruit. I glanced at the pans in the kitchen sink. No more oatmeal and no bacon for me. I sighed. It would be nice if my mother would recognize that girls can use a hot breakfast, too. I mean yogurt and fruit is okay for when I make breakfast, but why couldn't she make me a hot one like she made Eric? She's very sexist sometimes.

I sat in my usual spot, sort of across from Eric. My back was to the windows outside because Eric wouldn't ever sit there. He reads way too many crime novels, and good cops and PIs don't ever sit with their backs to the windows. As a result, I'm always sure there are werewolves or something creeping up through our yard ready to take me out.

I pushed those thoughts away. Given how I was feeling with the wish building, it would be just my luck that I'd grant a wish making a werewolf real.

We ate in silence but for slurps and crunches, mostly on Eric's part. The ripple of the pages Eric turned floated through the house. The ice maker dropped a few cubes and that was it. I got up and rinsed my dish and put in the sink, around all the pans Mom had used.

I like my brother, but it's not like we have a ton of stuff to say to each other. At least not since we outgrew picking on each other and making fun of each other. Eric could certainly be worse. I mean my friend Ashley's little brother is a royal pain who gets away with everything.

I hurried upstairs. I carefully packed my towel, more sunscreen, my phone, and everything else into my tote. I took the tote and went downstairs to get a water bottle.

"Morning Willow," my mother said. She was at the sink, filling it with soapy water to wash the dishes. We have a dishwasher, but it takes up more water, unless we fill it up completely, which we usually do at dinner time. But not breakfast.

"Morning." I grabbed my stainless steel water bottle that wasn't supposed to kill me, at least not today, and started filling it with ice and some water. When I went outside, the ice would melt pretty quickly, but I'd still have cool water. I considered taking some snacks. If I had to spend the day at the pool, I didn't want to be hungry.

"What are your plans?" my mom asked.

Eric got up and closed his book, bringing his dish to the sink and dropping it in.

"I have to go to class," he said, as if Mom were talking to him. He smirked at me.

I made a face at him.

"I was thinking of going back to the pool," I said.

My mom sighed.

I felt my wish power growing.

"What's with you and the pool? You stayed there nearly all day yesterday. That's unlike you."

Now see? That's totally my mom. One day she wishes I'd spend more time there and now she's worried because I'm spending too much time there. Some people should never have their wishes granted.

I spent a moment thinking about how the conversation would play out, "Well you see Mom, yesterday you wished that I would spend more time at the pool. I had a wish building. Normally that kind of thing wouldn't work because it was about me, but there are these sun spots so…"

And she'd stand there looking at me like I'd grown a third head or something.

Not that I could say that, because even if I tried, the words just wouldn't come out. I'd probably stand there with my mouth opening and closing like one of those stupid Big Mouth Bass fish that my grandpa has in his office.

"It just seems like something to do. You did say you wanted me to spend more time there," I said.

"But I didn't mean all the time." My mom rinsed off one of the pans.

Wishes absolutely do not care what you mean at all. Even when there aren't sun spots. Believe me.

I closed the water bottle and put it in my bag. I searched through the cupboards and found a few protein bars that my mom keeps. They're organic and supposed to be all natural and she says they're better for me than candy bars. I think they taste like dirt with a squirt of dog crap, but that's just me, or so my mom says. Still, they'd fill me up.

"You are taking sun screen aren't you?" My mom asked.

I nodded. I wanted to get upstairs and put on my music and hopefully avoid my mom long enough so I didn't grant her another stupid wish. She might wish I'd do more housework.

"Okay then. But try not to stay there so long."

I climbed the stairs. The wish pressure was building. I couldn't even believe that I was having to grant a wish two days in a row, especially when there were sun spots and I was supposed to be careful and try to avoid granting them during the day. This was just wrong.

I laid back on my bed and listened to music on my MP3 until I felt like I had to get to the pool.

Promptly at ten, when the pool opened, I had this urge to go running off. I tried to make myself move slowly. Sure, I had this urge to get to the pool, but I really didn't want to go, if you know what I mean. It was more of a compulsion. Considering how icky it felt, I doubt I'll end up one of those people who has to do things a certain way. Because ick.

I checked my phone as I went downstairs. Sage hadn't texted me yet, so I didn't send her a note. She wasn't likely to be happy about a second day at the pool, particularly with her sunburn. Fortunately, I'd just turned a little pink on my shoulders. Lobster is no one's favorite look.

I grabbed my bag and headed out. The wish pressure was making me feel bloated and icky. I put on my earbuds to listen to music. I walked to the pool this time rather than running. I felt weighted down, and I guess in a way I was. I needed to grant a wish, but I was hoping I wouldn't hear anything too big.

I grabbed the same chair I was in the day before. It would be nice and shady soon enough. I considered grabbing one by an umbrella so I could stay in the shade pretty much all day but I wasn't sure I wanted to. If Sage came, she would wonder why I was outside if I was in the shade. Getting a good tan in the shade takes way too long.

Of course it was already hot, humid, and suffocating. Sometimes I hate North Carolina. It was like moving through soup except, of course, it was easier to breathe, but only just. I pulled off my tank top, shorts, and earbuds, and got in the pool.

The water felt only a little cooler than the air, and only a little wetter. This was why I don't go to the pool more. It was only a little after ten in the morning and the pool felt like bath water.

It was a good day to stay inside. As much as I longed to do just that, Mom's wish was keeping me in the danged pool, so I paddled around. I didn't have the energy to do laps. I had to focus on a song playing in my head rather than listen to music from the safety of my room or even the lounger.

Without the music, I could totally hear people wishing. That's the thing about being a fairy godmother. You can hear things you shouldn't be able to hear. In fact, sometimes people don't even have to say the words "I wish" for me to hear them. Sometimes they just have to think them. It varies and I totally don't understand it.

The wish power meant I felt like I was swimming with this huge bowling bowl strapped to my middle. I worried it was going to drown me.

It is so hard to explain. I mean the wish power isn't like a weight, exactly, but it is. Brian, in my group, once described it as like having to fart. I think Grace described it as like having a baby. I haven't had a baby but I have had to fart—not that I'll ever admit I said that, just so you know—and it's got to be way more like having a baby than having to fart.

Farts don't have weight. Wishes did. And you had to push them out. It was like carrying something around in your belly area. How much more like being pregnant can you get?

Apparently wish pressure also makes you tired if you don't go out and grant one as soon as you start needing to, which was something I've never had to go through before. Fortunately. And, hopefully, it wasn't going to be like that every day.

I dove down to the deepest part of the pool, which is about five feet and change, although they claim it's six feet. I can almost stand on tip toe and I am not six feet tall.

I spent a good twenty minutes paddling around, mostly way underwater. Finally my wish-need to stay in the pool eased and I got out and laid out on the lounger to dry. I'd put more sun screen on in a few. I put my earbuds in quickly, just in case anyone had the poor taste to wish for something in my hearing.

Soon enough, even with the music, I was hearing wishes. I knew there was a thirty something woman waiting for her doctor and she was wishing they would hurry up. I quirked a smile at the thought of what bad things could happen. I pushed it down before I let any power go.

The wish pressure kept building. I needed to grant one. I searched through all the wishes that I was hearing and tried to latch onto one that seemed safe enough. None of them seemed really safe.

I wanted a kid with dog or something. Those are

usually the most straight-forward and the universe won't let you do much to those. And hey, if you got a zombie puppy, that's kind of cool too, right?

Okay, I know. Totally mean. But totally funny, too. If you're me.

I was kind of smiling at the thought when I heard this one wish come through. It was really strong.

"I wish I didn't have jury duty tomorrow."

And swish, the pink stuff flooded out of me. I wondered how that wish was going to manifest. Would she get a call because no one was having trials? It was hard to say. I settled back into my lounger much more comfortable.

My phone rang and the number was unfamiliar. I answered it with my best business-like voice, just in case. And yep. I had an interview. On Monday, around noon. At the local grocery store on the way to my dad's work. Five days away, pretty much. I hoped I could bank up enough pool time that I could go.

Chapter Six

Wishes don't care what you mean. — *Willow Vaughn*

I texted with Sage for a bit after that. I had to tell someone that I had gotten the interview, and it wasn't like the three moms sitting out by the pool were going to be all excited about me working. They were far too intent upon a discussion of baby food. What is it with moms and food?

Sage wanted me to go to the mall with her. I wanted to go. But the wish, the need to be at the pool, insisted I stay there. I felt like a prisoner.

I suggested we go later, hoping that I could force myself to leave. But no, she wanted to go over lunch time.

Which meant she was hoping to see Doug Layton. He was working at some sporting goods store at the mall—I mean his senior year he was the quarterback of the football team, so you sort of expect him to know about sports equipment, right? Sage had a crush on him.

My brother is a good friend of Doug's. Doug and I are just friends, because, like, you just can't see a guy that way if you know him the way I do. I know Sage was hoping that if she was eating alone he might join her. It would be better with me because, like I said, Doug and I were friends and he'd at least come say hello. And I could yell 'hello' if she wanted to act like she didn't see him.

But no. I was stuck at the pool.

I fidgeted around the lounger and finally felt the need to get back in the water. I swam around for a little while. It felt good to be able to move again but I was bored. I wanted to be at the mall, looking at clothes or even eating bad food and having a soda. It would be cooler there and I'd have someone to talk to. Because, like, right now, my conversational options were the mom's talking about poop and baby food.

It was enough to make me think about never having children.

I settled back on the lounger and listened to music. I probably dozed off a couple of times. I kept rotating which side was in the sun so I didn't burned. At around three I felt like I could leave, having given the pool another shot. Hopefully I'd used enough sun screen.

I dressed quickly. I tried calling my mom, but she wasn't answering her cell phone. I figured she was talking to one of her friends about whether she needed to volunteer at the homeless ostrich shelter or something.

I was hungry so I hurried home, although the black top was scalding, even through my flip flops. Like, my mom is always around but now when she'd be useful…

This was why I needed a car.

Mom wasn't home when I got there, which was no surprise. I rinsed out my bathing suit in the sink and then went down and made myself a sandwich. I took the plate upstairs with me and ate while messing on my computer.

Sage texted me. She had eaten alone. Doug had seen

her and waved but he didn't come over to talk to her. She was really bummed about that.

That was my fault of course.

I felt bad for letting my friend down. I wished I could at least explain. I mean if I had had to work at least Sage would have understood.

As it was, it's not like I could explain what really happened with my mom's wish. Although I could totally see Sage laughing at me if I tried to explain it.

At first, I wasn't too worried about where my Mom was. She might have taken up buffalo hide weaving for all I knew. Not, of course, that there were buffalos in North Carolina, but it's the idea. If there was a buffalo, and it donated some sort of wool for spinning, trust me, my mom would find it.

But as the time inched closer to dinner and she wasn't back, I started to wonder what was wrong.

A little after five, which is later than my mom normally starts dinner, I heard the garage door go up. I came out of my room to hurry downstairs to grill her on where she'd been. I mean, if I learned nothing else from her, I learned how to grill someone who is late.

But it wasn't my mother coming into the kitchen. It was my dad.

"Where's Mom?" I asked.

"What?" He seemed surprised that she wasn't home.

He pulled out his cell phone and tried to call her.

He looked at the phone oddly.

"What?" I asked.

"It's not going through?" He seemed puzzled. He tried again. This time he smiled and nodded.

"Where are you?" he asked abruptly, so my mom must have picked up.

"What?... Hmm... Yes... Yes... Be careful... No we're

fine here... I didn't have any problems... I'm sure Eric's fine... No... Be careful... Don't worry..."

Finally he closed the phone, an odd look on his face. My father is not normally given to expressiveness. He's the only reason I believe that someone wouldn't ever roll their eyes. Because he wouldn't. It's not that he's serious. He makes jokes all the time. It's just that he doesn't look like he's laughing. He'll be there completely serious and start talking about something ridiculous.

But right now he looked like he didn't know if he was worried or if he was going to burst out laughing.

"What?" I asked.

"Your mom was sorting clothing for the shelter, you know, the one that's attached to the back of the building that houses city hall and the courthouse," he said.

I nodded. I'd been forced to help sometimes. Not something I really wanted to, do but my mom thought it was good for me. It's in this funny annex towards the back of the city hall that looks like someone built a lean-to up against the bigger building because it's so much smaller. It's right by the bus stop and there's a thrift store across the street.

"I guess there was some sort of explosion in the courthouse. At first they were worried it was a bomb, but I guess the water main backed up and all the toilets exploded. One toilet flew up so high it broke through two ceilings above it, and nearly hit a judge. I guess the structure is pretty damaged so they weren't letting anyone back inside," my dad said.

I just looked at him with my mouth open. When does something like that happen?

"They cordoned off the area so your mom couldn't even get to her car for a long time, and now the traffic is a mess," my dad finished. He sort of snorted at the end of that.

It was funny. I mean, toilets? Exploding?

I was thinking about the wish I'd granted to the woman who wanted out of jury duty.

I mean, come on. Exploding toilets? This was so not a normal thing. It totally had to be because of that wish. I mean, if a toilet flew up through the floor of the building, it wasn't like the jurors were going to have to be called for jury duty tomorrow which fulfilled her wish. Probably for a good long time.

"What do you want to do for dinner?" my father asked me. "Eric should be home soon but we're the ones who get to pick."

I shrugged. I really wanted to go upstairs and read more about the whole exploding toilet thing. I kind of wanted to look up and see how often toilets exploded, too. Just in case I was wrong and it wasn't the wish. Maybe they explode and injure people more often than I thought.

Chapter Seven

Meditation can help fairy godmothers focus on a wish that needs to be granted — The Fairy Godmother Handbook

Mom came home close to seven. My dad had decided on pizza, which is a major treat for all of us. Mom doesn't much like take-out pizza. We all ate our share, talking about the exploding toilet.

"Did they come to you for plumbing help?" My dad kidded Eric.

Eric snorted. "It wouldn't have happened if they had. I'm the plumbing king!"

I giggled but didn't add much to the conversation. By the time Mom walked in, we were done eating and putting the extra pizza away, while making jokes about what might have come out of the toilet.

We all practically jumped on her to tell us what had happened.

I had to admit, my mom looked a bit the worse for wear. Her hair was kind of wetted down around her head and at first I worried she'd gotten sprayed with the toilet water—EWW!—but she was just hot.

They'd been stuck outside around the building and there wasn't any place to go to wait that had air conditioning, at least not by the time my mom thought of it. She'd been so hot, she'd even purchased bottled water, which is like saying the world nearly ended for her because, you know, bottles from bottled water pollute.

While she pulled out the leftover pizza and sat down to talk to my dad, I went upstairs to google what else was going on. This could not all be about me. It had to be the sun spots, so hopefully there were weird things happening all over.

In California there had been a weird little rainstorm just over a garden. There was a video of the newscaster standing there, showing the wet spot on the ground and the neighbors and the homeowner saying that a cloud had come up and it had rained for a good three minutes just over that one spot.

No one had a video though.

Which meant I was skeptical but not as much as I would have been if the sun spots hadn't been making wishes act weird.

I had until to Monday to wonder, though. Then I could ask the others about what was happening. But even then, I'd have to get through another week of trying not to mess up too badly.

Then I climbed into bed and drifted off dreaming about men setting toilets to explode all over Charlotte. I was running around, terrified that I had to stop it and fix them. I have no idea what would happen if I didn't. I was tired when I woke up, and kind of worried that I was taking this wish thing a little too seriously.

I mean dreaming about exploding toilets? Seriously?

I made my usual breakfast. My mom was at the table having tea. This told me she was kind of upset about what happened. I guess if you think it's a bomb, that's pretty scary, even if it ends up just being a toilet.

"Morning," I said. I set down my bowl of yogurt and berries, which were blueberries today because there were no raspberries. I also had more walnuts.

"Morning," my mom said. "What are your plans for today?"

I shrugged. "I thought maybe I'd go back out to the pool and listen to some music."

Mom sighed. "What is it with you and the pool this year? Last year you'd go a couple times a week for maybe an hour, and this year it's like you live there."

I shrugged. "You said get out of the house. Maybe I like it."

Mom made a face at me. "Be careful."

Seriously? There were two or three lifeguards on every shift. I couldn't drown myself if I wanted to. Of course, maybe she was worried that the pool toilets would explode or something. Not that exploding toilets are all that common. At least not according to the internet.

I ate my breakfast. Mom sipped her tea, not saying much.

I got up and put the dish in the sink.

"Willow!" my mom kind of yelled. It was more that why-can't-you-do-something-right voice.

"What?" I asked.

"Why can't you put water in that dish so nothing sticks to it?"

I looked down. There was water in the dish. Granted I hadn't washed it-washed it but it was sort of wet and there was water standing in it.

I sighed, loudly, and went back and rubbed the edges

of the dish and made sure it was mostly clean so she wouldn't have to work so hard to clean it. Not that it was hard to clean or anything. In fact, I could have put it in the drying rack, but she gets mad when I do that, because the dishes, although clean to the eye, are not clean enough. Germs. Microbes.

The whole germ thing makes no sense to me at all. She makes me take probiotics, which are just bacteria, and she's terrified of something on a plate. Germs. Which are probably bacteria. Hello, Mom!

I stomped up the stairs to show my displeasure, laid back on my bed, and felt a wish starting to build. This one wasn't as heavy as the one yesterday. Maybe it would build slower and I could get to the evening time so I wouldn't cause any more toilets to explode.

I giggled a little.

So far, I wasn't hearing any wishes too loudly. I mean, there was the lady down the way yelling at her dogs that she wished they'd shut up, but I didn't feel an urge to grant that wish. The way things were going, the dogs would die. I'd feel bad about that. Not for the lady yelling, you understand, but for the dogs. The dogs hadn't done anything except try and get her attention and she was just yelling at them. I knew exactly how that felt.

I got up to mess on the computer. I read about sun spots, or tried to. There was nothing that was interesting, and nothing on any of the sites that explained what might be going on to make them suddenly interfere with magic. Not that I seriously thought there were sites that would explain how sunspots interfered with magic.

As near as I could tell there were always sun spots. It was just that sometimes they got more active. They had some sort of magnetic resonance or something but I could be wrong about that because I'm so not super good at science and I wasn't totally sure I understood it all. While I love watching Abby on NCIS and think it's totally cool that she knows all that science stuff, I am so not her. And not just because I have no desire to sleep in a coffin.

That made me wonder if anyone had ever tested the magic we used as fairy godmothers. I looked through the manual. Naturally it wasn't helpful. I had to wonder if it would have killed whoever wrote the manual to make it interesting. It's totally Snore City.

I did notice that someone had added a chapter on how not to hear a wish so you could avoid granting it. That hadn't been there a few months ago. I would know. I looked.

When it got close to ten I started getting antsy about going to the pool. I made a face as I packed up my bag and got out of there. I had no enthusiasm for sitting around outside and listening to music again. I mean, yeah, I like music, and the outdoors is fine, but I'd been doing that. Every. Single. Day.

I opened front door and a blast of oven warm heat pushed me back in. It was going to suck walking over to the pool. In fact, it was pretty much going to suck being outside all day. I had some water, but I doubted that would be enough. Maybe the wish would let me come in early. I'd already spent more time at the pool this week than I normally did.

I trudged through the heat. It was so hot I thought I could smell the asphalt baking. I knew I could smell myself, despite the deodorant I used that morning. Imagine what I'd smell like after a few hours in this.

I showed my ID and got my usual chair. I didn't even sit down before I picked up and moved to a chair with an umbrella that would keep me in the shade all day. I so didn't want to be out. If there were a breeze or anything, it wouldn't be nearly so bad.

It was so hot, all I could think of was that if the toilets exploded here, at least there would be cool water pouring down on us. Even if it was totally gross.

I climbed into the pool. With the heat, it smelled more like chlorine than ever, and it felt like getting into a warm bath. Thankfully it was not yet up to hot bath temperature, just warmer than I'd like in the hot weather.

There were more people around, moms getting little kids into the pool, so that later on, when it got really hot, they could all be inside. I'd love to know that I was going to get to go back inside. A woman with a bathing cap and sun glasses was doing the breast stroke back and forth in the pool near the side closest to the life guard.

The morning crawled. I have had math classes that didn't drag like this. At least the classroom didn't feel like an oven. I have never been so bored. Except maybe that one time my mom took me out to her friend Yvonne's to watch her shear goats. Yes, literally shear goats. Really.

Finally, as the clock ticked towards two, I was able to pull myself off the lounger. I was so hot, I felt kind of nauseous. I wasn't sure I'd be able to leave, thanks to the wish, but I could, probably because the wish power knew my body couldn't take any more heat. If feeling kind of like I could vomit any time wasn't bad enough, the wish cramp was starting to get bigger.

I needed a shower. A cold one. And a large cold glass of water. I'd prefer a soda or something with sugar, but we don't have that in the house.

My mom didn't answer her cell phone, so I had to walk home in the heat, which did not feel good, believe me. She wanted me to go to the pool more often, but then she's never around to pick me up when it's hot. A car would be so useful.

"It's about time!" my mom sang out from somewhere in the house. She was probably in the kitchen, trimming her herbs. It was Thursday, and she usually went through and made sure all the indoor herbs were looking okay on Thursday afternoons. My mother likes routine. She says it keeps her on track.

I hurried up the stairs. In my room I peeled everything off. I grabbed a robe and went to the bathroom for a cool shower.

In the mirror my face was a bright cherry red from the heat. I looked as wrecked as I felt. It was a good thing my mom hadn't come out from the kitchen, because one look and she'd have been so pissed-off at me.

As I started to cool off, I felt a little better, though I still felt weird in my stomach and wanted to eat something.

The wish cramp was getting stronger. I was so going to need to listen to music for the rest of the afternoon. I went downstairs and made myself a sandwich while my mom continued playing with her herbs.

She was cooking something in a big pot as well, which could have been anything from bone broth to spaghetti sauce. I didn't ask which. Whatever it was, it hadn't been cooking long enough to create a smell to overpower the scent of the trimmed rosemary that threatened to crawl up my nose and die.

I ate quietly, listening to music, and then I went back upstairs to lie on my bed and concentrate on the beat. I was starting to hear things like "I wish it were dinner time." Would their dinner magically appear earlier or would time move forward? Hard to know and not a chance I wanted to take.

Not after the exploding toilet fiasco.

People were wishing for the day to end (so not going there), their boss to get off their back (now that was an interesting image) and for their child to get home. They were wishing to have phone calls returned and to get that job. I was doing a good job of ignoring them.

I bopped away on my bed, listening to music and texting to my friends. We were setting up plans for what we'd do at Ashley's tomorrow evening. I made a list of things I should bring, and reminded myself to tell my mom where I'd be, because she'd be pissed off at me if I didn't warn her.

And then, there it was. A wish so small I didn't have to ignore it. It was four in the afternoon and the sun was still pretty high in the sky and I had hoped to make it until dark or at least close to dark but this was such an easy wish, what could go wrong?

"I wish I had a bike." A little kid. Should have been simple. *Bam,* I was on the roof top of her house and sent out the pink cloud. I didn't have a choice, but better to aim it well rather than let it go where it wanted. After all, maybe my aim was half the problem.

And there, suddenly, in her driveway sat a Harley Davidson.

A bike.

The kid was maybe eight at the most.

Not exactly the bike she wished for.

I started to giggle so hard I nearly fell off the roof.

Okay, at least there were no exploding toilets with this wish. At least I wasn't stuck riding the damned bike either.

I jumped back to my room and lay on my bed laughing to myself.

"Are you okay in there, Willow?" my mom asked, tapping on the door.

"I'm fine," I said. "A joke online."

"I think you spend too much time online."

At least I didn't have a wish pressure building, in case she said she wished I didn't spend so much time online. Who knew when I'd get back to the computer then, particularly since I wasn't even using it?

"What would you like me to do?" I yelled through the door. "Go back to the pool?"

"At least you're outside in the fresh air. Maybe you could go for a walk."

I heard her walk down the hallway.

Go for a walk? What did she think I was? Sixty? Who went walking? In this heat?

I shook my head wondering what my mom was even thinking. Sometimes I think all that organic food has made her a bit crazy.

I went back to listening to music and texting my friends. For the first time in my life I wished I could tell people about being a fairy godmother.

Chapter Eight

Being a fairy godmother is work — *Willow Vaughn*

Friday was a lot like Thursday. I hung out at the pool, tried to ignore wish pressure, and not be too bored. I listened to my music and texted with my friends while enjoying the enchanting scent of chlorine, because, well, it's hard to keep the pool from growing gross things when it's a hundred degrees out.

I hoped that I wouldn't have to go to the pool on Saturday when I was at Ashley's. Maybe distance would mitigate the need to be there? Because if not, how was I going to explain that I needed to leave that early just to go to the pool?

This was the worst wish ever.

At home, I put together the stuff I would need to go to Ashley's. I'd remembered to tell my mom and, as I suspected, she was okay with me going. I was packing a fresh pair of under things when I found I had packed my bathing suit. We weren't going to go swimming, but I was putting in there. I pulled it out.

I packed toiletries and once again, I found my bathing suit in the bag. I couldn't even remember putting it in there! I had to wonder if the wish was just making the suit walk over and climb into the bag on its own.

Now that was creepy.

What was worse, my bathing suit was wet.

"Okay. So this is wet. It needs to dry. Otherwise how will I wear it?" I asked, out loud. I have no idea who I was talking to. But at least I was able to pack normally without pulling the bathing suit out every two minutes.

Suddenly the wish cramp came on big and strong. It does that sometimes. This one nearly doubled me over.

I started thinking up good excuses in case my mom walked in. She worries. In fact, if she didn't have something real to worry about, she'd make something up. Me doubled over would about send us off to the emergency room, if she couldn't get a hold of her naturopath, and that so did not sound like fun. Plus, I could kiss Ashley's sleepover good bye.

I got to my bed and curled up around my belly, as if I were just listening to music and maybe feeling a little sleepy. My mom would still worry, but she probably wouldn't think I was dying.

I started searching around for a wish.

"I wish he liked me…" I tossed that aside.

"I wish I had her hair…" another toss aside, although momentarily tempting.

"I wish I'd never met him…" so tossed that aside. Bad wish. Not that there were any good wishes at this point in time and if there were, somehow the sun spots were likely to make them bad.

"I wish I won…" Too vague. I wasn't going to take a chance.

"I wish I could buy a house…" I felt drawn to that. I

popped out to a downtown somewhere. Not sure where, but it certainly wasn't Charlotte.

It was this run-down sort of downtown. An old sign hung down at an angle from a post and when the breeze—thankfully cool—came through, it sent it squeaking when it moved. The sidewalk was cracked, and the road had so many potholes I couldn't imagine how you'd drive down it.

A laundromat had lights on, and an older woman was in there pulling out clothing. A few doors down was a real estate agency. Inside were two people. One of them was a sort of ageless man with black hair, slicked back. He didn't smile, but I could feel the need coming off of him. He was super thin and super pale, like maybe he was a vampire, although the sun was still up.

I sent out the pink cloud towards the man in the office, hoping that would send me back home.

The place was super creepy. I was just glad it wasn't night, because all I could think of was that I'd just granted a wish for Dracula to buy a house. Maybe I'd gone to Transylvania, and that's why things looked so old and broken down.

But I had been able to read the signs, and I didn't think that they wrote in English in Transylvania. I just hoped that wherever I had been, the guy wasn't going to be setting up a house and making everyone vampires. Because wouldn't that be something for Stephen King to write about?

Even so, I was really glad I didn't have any wish pressure to carry around when I went to the sleep over.

At least now I could totally have a good time. If Saturday morning rolled around and changed that, well, I'd worry about that then.

My mom was nice enough to drive me and Sage over to Ashley's at five. We were eating at her place, probably ordering in. Ashley's mom is so much nicer than mine about food.

We didn't talk much on the way over because my mom was there. It would be so much better when I could afford to buy my own car. I just needed that job. I was going to be so pissed off with my mom if she ruined that for me because I had to stay at the pool rather than go to an interview.

"Call me and I'll come by and get you," my mom said. "And if you're going to be later than noon, call me and let me know. Ashley's parents can bring you back if it's that late."

"Great." I closed the door, careful not to slam it and piss my mother off so I'd get a finger shaking. Then she'd probably demand I come back so she could change the time to ten instead of noon which meant I'd have to wake up early and battle the pool compulsion.

"I can't believe how tan you are," Sage said. "What have you been doing?"

"Avoiding my mom," I said. "She's got a bunch of worry bees up her butt, so I've been hanging at the pool. I'm starting to like it a little, I guess. Especially early when everyone isn't there yet."

Sage shrugged, but at least I'd given her an excuse she'd buy. I mean she knows my mom and how she can get.

Lauren was already there, slumped over on the sofa in the upstairs media room. My folks have a room upstairs that's sort of a rec room, but it's not nearly as nice as this. Ashley's folks had decorated it in Panther blue and had a ton of pennants and posters around the room. About a foot from the ceiling, there were shelves of bobble-head dolls and other what-nots.

The beige microfiber sofa wasn't really a sofa, but a

group of reclining chairs that had cup holders in-between. They were really comfortable, and we'd slept in them more than once. Everything was really tidy.

Ashley's brother, Troy, was there, of course. He's annoying but at least he's a known quantity. At least for sleepovers, her parents actually wanted him to join them for dinner, so we had a little time without him annoying us. It's like the only time they think Ashley might enjoy not having her brother around. Otherwise he always gets to do whatever he wants, which is usually tormenting Ashley.

True to form, we got to order pizza and watch movies on Netflix while we gossiped about people in school.

I scarfed down my pepperoni and mushroom pizza. We got mushrooms so I could tell my mom that there was a vegetable on it. Ashley and Sage pulled them off. I like them. And I had a soda. No need to tell my mom about that. She's under the impression that we get healthy drinks from one of the in-home soda makers where we combine fruit juices and carbonated water.

I'm surprised that she and Ashley's mom, who are friendly, haven't talked about the fact that that thing hasn't worked in over a year.

"What'cha watching?" Troy bounced into the room. He grabbed a piece of pizza from the table on the far side of our chairs and was shoving it into his mouth before anyone could stop him.

"You had your own damned pizza," Ashley screamed. "How dare you?"

Troy laughed and bounced back out of the room.

Ashley got up and slammed the door closed. She even moved one of those roller carts in front of it. It wasn't likely to keep Troy out, but would give us warning if he tried to come back in.

"I hate him," Ashley swore.

I was so glad I didn't have a wish push building. Because one time she'd wished he hadn't ever been born, and that had been a nightmare. If I accidentally granted that wish again, sun spots or no, there would be no going back. I *so* did not like that world.

So we gossiped and watched a movie and then gossiped some more. Lauren had a new makeup thing we all had to try on our eyes. It was a way of using multiple colors of eyeshadow and blending them. I used blues and greens because I have sort of green hazel eyes.

"It's awesome-looking," Lauren said looking at me. "You normally can't wear blue at all but this is just perfect."

I had to admit it did seem to make my eye color stand out. The green shadow was just enough, and the blue subtle enough, that I didn't look like I was going for a retro look.

Ashley wasn't as successful with the browns and lavenders she was using. Lauren came over and smeared it a little more and that made her eyes look great.

All that done, we went back for another movie. It wasn't that late, and what else were we going to do all night?

Finally, even we had to wind down and fall asleep, which we did. Ashley made sure the cart was in front of the door as we all started getting tired because there was no way we wanted Troy coming in.

I'm not sure who dropped off first, but I know I was the first one to wake up. It was nine in the morning, or close to that, and I was itching to pull on my bathing suit and get to the pool. I tried to doze back off, thinking that I could go later, but the compulsion was having none of my logic.

I probably would have called my mom, but I got

another wish cramp. I wondered what kind of a mess I was going to make now.

I tried to listen for good wishes, but all the ones I could hear were all for big things.

As the cramp got larger I got up to use the rest room so I could be alone for a second. Once in there, I did my business and then turned the water on. While washing my hands, I said out loud, "I wish I didn't feel a need to go to the pool all the time."

I put all my will into sending out wish-granting mojo, but there was no pink cloud and no easing of my cramps. I clearly couldn't grant my own wishes, sun spots or not.

It was worth the try. I slipped back into the room. Lauren stirred, but then went back to sleep.

I crawled back into my chair and closed my eyes, trying to relax. As pool opening time got closer and closer, I felt it pulling on me. I was going to miss getting my favorite lounger. I needed to call my mom and make sure my bathing suit was dry. I should be there. It would get too crowded and I'd miss out. I'd be sorry if I didn't go. I had to be there. Who knew what I'd see? What if there was a cute boy?

But the pressure was on. I did my best to ignore it.

At the same time, I kept listening for a safe wish. You know, like someone wishing for pancakes for breakfast or for a kitten or a puppy.

I shuddered when someone said "I wish I was dead." I could grant that. I had to grab onto my wish power to make sure it didn't go out. That scared me a lot.

"I wish it would cool off." How bad would I mess up if I messed with the weather I wondered?

I didn't want to grant the wish but I'd popped out before I could think. Probably because I wished it would cool off, too. So there I was, standing in a shaded area in an older part of town. At least I had stayed in Charlotte this time. I could tell by the skyline to the east.

I sent off pink clouds of wish juju towards the old woman who was wishing. She was walking very slowly down the street with a walker. She was in a sort of sleeveless shift in pale blue, and her dark skin was beaded with sweat. She was with an older man in light slacks and a short-sleeved shirt. He was carrying a bag of something.

Before I popped out, I saw the sky darkening. It looked like it was about to rain and rain hard. Great.

I was back in my chair when hail started to rain down on the roof of Ashley's house. That woke up Lauren, who looked around perplexed.

She met my gaze. I shrugged. She got out of the middle chair, where she always sat, next to Ashley, and looked out the window.

"Holy shit," she swore.

"What?" I got up to look out.

It was hailing like crazy. The trees were bending under the wind. I knew that just a few minutes ago it had been hotter than heck. I hoped the older people had gotten to shelter some place before this came on. It had happened to so fast.

It was really bothering me that they were outside. I hadn't noticed a place to huddle against the rain or hail or whatever. They had looked a bit frail. Were they okay? And what kind of a wish had I granted this time? How long would it last?

The woman had just said she wished it would cool off.

Even as I watched, the hail started to turn to snow.

Chapter Nine

When granted correctly, wishes give the wish granter a good feeling —
The Fairy Godmother Handbook

Ashley and Sage woke up when it started to thunder. Who knew you could have thunder snow, I mean outside Minnesota, but that's, like, *Minnesota?*

"What's going on?" Sage yawned and stretched. She looked around and finally saw Lauren and me standing there, looking out the window.

It was snowing so hard that I couldn't see across the street. The people across the street had had a gray car in their driveway but now it was covered with piles of white.

"It's snowing?" Lauren said. She seemed really perplexed.

"It's July," Sage said, starting to get up, but not really paying attention to the window.

The door banged open. Troy. The cart squealed as it rolled away and then banged into the wall, adding another shudder to the house.

"Isn't this the coolest?" He was practically jumping up and down. He rushed over to the window with us.

The window was fogging up and I couldn't even see the tree across the way. The ceiling creaked weirdly, like there was something heavy on it.

I wondered how cold it had gotten and what that would do to the older people walking down the road. It wasn't like they were dressed for this.

Sage had gotten up and come over to the window. Even Ashley was waking up, frowning.

I tried to look out and see what was going on, but the window was all white, like snow had covered it. We were on the second floor, so nothing could have come down that fast. At least I didn't think so.

"Why don't you girls come down for breakfast," Ashley's mom said. "I'm not sure if we'll have power long with this storm, so let's get started now."

I was only too happy to go. Ashley practically leaped out of her chair and followed her mom. Sage and Lauren trailed after us. Troy remained upstairs until we got down into the big galley kitchen and Ashley's dad called up to him.

Ashley's parents had already started cooking up breakfast. Bacon was sizzling away, nearly done. There was even a pile of pancakes on a plate. We all took some. There was real maple syrup. While Ashley's mother isn't as bad as mine—no one is—she'd been around my mom enough that she buys some of the good stuff.

It was a good breakfast, and we ate in the large kitchen nook that serves as their dining room. The kitchen dumps out into this large square room with a big bay window that takes up the whole back wall. Beyond the eating area is the main family room with the family television and two big gray blue sofas that don't recline.

I got to sit across from the bay window, so I got to watch the snow—except, of course, that it was coming down so fast, it was like seeing a white curtain outside.

Down here we heard wind coming through the kitchen vents. It wasn't just snowing, it was windy, too.

I heard something crack, the sound coming from the front room. I paused, fork full of pancakes halfway to my mouth.

"What's that?" Ashley asked quietly.

Then there was a loud crash.

"Stay here," her father said, getting up. He was dressed and even had on slippers with leather soles on them. The rest of us were all barefoot.

I shivered feeling a cold wind come through the house. It wasn't me. Everyone else was shivering, too.

"Front window broke," he said.

"Cool!" Troy said. He started to get up and go look out.

"Stay here," his mother said. "You're barefoot, and we aren't going out to the doctor in this. We don't know how long it will last."

"I'll go look in the garage to see if there's something to cover the opening," Ashley's father said. He was running his hand through his dark hair, doing all the things dads did when they were worried and didn't want to admit it.

I went back to eating, even though my stomach didn't feel good about this.

It was weird. When I'd granted some not-so-good wishes before, I felt it right away. I didn't feel this right away at all. I mean, I felt badly *now*, but it was more thinking that this storm was my fault for granting that wish. It wasn't that icky, uh-oh feeling I got when I accidentally granted a wish I shouldn't have.

Then I wondered why I thought this was my fault. I

mean can't people be more responsible for what they wish for? Why do I have to police what they wish for all the time? It's ridiculous.

I finished my pancakes and bacon. Lauren did, too, although Sage was still picking at hers, but that's pretty normal for her. Ashley had hardly touched her food. Sometimes she's like that. Or maybe the storm was scaring her.

Ashley's dad came through with a large board that Troy had used when he thought he wanted to do skateboard tricks. We all stood up and followed him to the doorway, hovering behind Ashley's mom who was picking her way through the room to try and help him.

He had to push himself forward, bent down against the wind, which kept threatening to tear the wood from his hands. Papers were strewn all over the room, and one of the pictures on the wall above the sofa was completely ruined. I wondered how our house had fared.

Snow was starting to pile up in front of the broken window. A tree branch was sort of waving a little bit near the floor, so it must have broken and then come through the window. I thought it looked kind of like the arm of a person buried in an avalanche.

My house had a ton of trees, which meant that windows could be knocked out all over the place. I wondered what my mother was doing. She's always going on about global warming and climate change. Probably talking more about the second than the first today.

I considered calling my mom. Thinking about her, thinking about connecting with her, I got this urge to go to the pool. Like, really? We have feet of snow in minutes, and there are windows breaking, and we're all standing around freezing, and I want to go to the pool? How crazy is that?

I went back to watching Ashley's dad fighting with the

board. My battle with the pool compulsion was kind of like that. Pushing forward only to get pushed back. Finally getting it in place and then trying to nail it up.

He was successful and got to rest. I just got restless.

Chapter Ten

Fairy Godmothers will meet weekly with their group — The Fairy Godmother Handbook

The snow went on for maybe another hour. By eleven my mom was on the phone calling to make sure I was okay.

I wasn't at all surprised that she showed up three seconds after snowmagedden stopped. Sage and I were ready to go. While we might have hung around to make plans for something else in the afternoon, none of us were likely to go anywhere but home. The snow was already melting, but who knew if it would continue to melt, or if it would melt so quickly roads would start to flood.

I sort of wanted to get home to my computer so I could look up more news on the weather. I wanted to see if anyone in downtown had gotten caught in the snow and had to be unfrozen. And maybe, just maybe, I could go to the pool.

While our house hadn't sustained any damage, our

cherry tree was bare and three limbs had fallen in our yard. It looked like a bunch of zombies had gone running through and left a bunch of human arms the way the reddish leaves were splashed all over the place.

A large river, almost a waterfall was running down Sage's driveway.

"How am I supposed to get up there?" she cried.

Her father was standing at the top of their driveway and he splashed down the drive to get her. Water came up to his ankles and there was still snow on the lawn.

Usually I liked snow, but this was not ordinary snow. I wondered what the weather channels were saying about this freak storm.

A breeze came up and it was still cold. I shivered in the chill. Well, at least the woman downtown had gotten her wish. I just hoped she had lived through it.

Sage's dad and my dad took her stuff up the driveway, walking carefully through the falling water.

"I feel like I'm up in the mountains," Sage's dad laughed. "Climbing up a waterfall."

My dad chuckled as he went up with Sage's sleeping bag. Sage followed right behind, trying not to get too wet. Of course, she was in shorts and sandals.

"It's so cold!" she called. At the top of the drive, she turned back to me and waved.

I went inside and up to my room, thankful that it was warm. I sat down at my computer and started looking for news.

Lots of news on the "freak storm" and some good photos. There were a couple of destroyed roofs because of the weight of the snow. One guy had the back of his pickup crushed. A ton of cars were parked beside the roads, with people inside, practically buried in the snow.

News footage showed people huddling together in

coffee shops. I thought I saw the old woman who had made the wish, but I couldn't be absolutely certain.

Another image showed a pool covered in ice and snow. Still another showed a pool overflowing as the snow melted. That made me want to go jump in. Which just pissed me off. I am *so* not a polar bear!

If only I could scream at my mom about ruining my life. I mean, let's get real.

There was a picture of a kids building a fort with snow. They even had on winter jackets. At least someone was prepared.

Two more days, I reminded myself. Then I could talk about my worries and see if anyone else was having major issues with wishes.

I noticed that in California, just outside of Sacramento, a new stand of redwoods had suddenly burst up and were now blocking the entrance to a subdivision.

In some tiny town in Russia everyone had turned pink and their faces had blown up and gotten real round. There were photos, and it looked like everyone had decided to do themselves up like a Hello Kitty cartoon. I started to laugh.

Clearly a lot of people were having wishes go wrong, so at least it wasn't just me.

I decided to go searching through the world news to see if I could figure out what the others had been doing. There was a lot of freak weather. A fishing boat had to call the Coast Guard because one of their fishing clients had caught such a large fish that the boat started sinking. *Definitely a wish gone bad*, I thought. At least that was relatively harmless. Everyone, except the fish, was okay.

I cheered myself with that and couldn't wait to hear stories on Monday. I had several to tell people myself. The fish story and my Harley story were both kind of awesome.

Two days. Probably two more wishes, although I could

hope that I'd be out of them for a while. I could hold out for two more days, right?

Chapter Eleven

The need to grant a wish is different each time — The Fairy Godmother's Handbook

Sage and I had planned to go out to a movie on Saturday and maybe grab a burger, but there was no way my mom was letting me go out. For once I was sort of agreeing with her. I mean, the snow was almost melted off, but there were still huge streams running down the roads and a there were more than a few branches lying across the street.

"My mom's afraid there'll be another storm," I told Sage. We were in our rec room upstairs, watching a Netflix movie on the smaller television. Sage was dressed in jeans and a sweatshirt, like she might wear in the winter, even though it was really warm outside already.

"I froze this morning," Sage had said when I looked surprised to see her dressed for winter. Not that I'm like judging. I wasn't wearing shorts either.

"What do you think happened?" Sage asked. "I mean

normally it doesn't just snow in Charlotte, and never in the summer!"

"No clue. I sort of listened to the news, but they didn't have any idea. All they can say is 'freak storm' and must have something to do with climate change and the water currents or something."

Sage nodded. "I know they were saying all kinds of things, but this was just way too weird."

We ate some chopped vegetables that my mom had put out. She'd made parsnip chips, which are okay sometimes, and talked about boys. Sage was pouting because she hadn't gotten to see Doug.

"We so could have gone by the store to see if he were working," she said. The theater we had planned to go to was across the parking lot from the mall.

I agreed, but really, what can you do? My brother was outside playing, although according to him he was measuring the water running down the street, like he knew anything about that. I think he just wanted to float things and see how fast they went down the road. That is so my brother. Normally Doug would have joined him, and that's probably why Sage had come over to watch movies, but Doug had to work.

Still, we made the best of it.

After Sage left, I read a little more news online. Seattle had had a tornado that made this stone statue called the Fremont Troll disappear. Nothing else was hurt. Probably a wish gone bad, especially since when you saw pictures it was this huge stone thing huddling under a bridge.

There was a tidal wave that hit Chile. Couldn't tell if that had anything to do with a wish or not. A house in Australia was overrun by snakes. At first I was sure that was a wish, but then I started reading up on Australia because I wanted to know what kind of wish caused that, really, and

I decided it might have been natural. Australia had a lot of nasty creatures, and I decided that if I ever traveled, I was so not going there.

I went to bed not long after that and dreamed of snakes. As tired as I was after the slumber party, I slept badly.

When I woke up Sunday I was grumpy. Mostly granting wishes made me feel good, but with all the wishes and the worry about the sunspots, I was going back to my regular cynical self. Because, like, nothing was really working out right at all. Except the kid who got the Harley, and even that was more of a mean happy than a good happy.

Oddly, I kind of missed being hopeful and happy, which was like the totally weirdest thing ever.

The sun was shining and you could really see all the broken branches, and I think the neighbors next to Sage had had the roof on their garage cave in. That would totally suck. But they were all out there, and someone was yelling really loudly which is what probably woke me up in the first place.

I stomped down stairs to get something to eat. My mom was in the kitchen with my dad and she was making eggs. Which meant I was having eggs. No bacon today.

"Eric doesn't have to work today, does he?" I asked.

"He got quite a chill when he was outside last night," my mom said. "I suggested he sleep in today."

Miracles never cease. I wondered if she took note of the dark circles under my eyes. Eric she'd let sleep. Me, she'd probably drive to an early grave with questions about why I couldn't sleep. This assumed that her pool wish didn't kill me first.

I sat down and started eating the eggs, to which she'd added a bit of spinach trimmed into little tiny pieces and feta cheese, when I got seized by this huge wish cramp. And I mean huge. Normally it feels like a cramp in my lower belly, like menstrual cramps. But this. This was something else. It was like my whole body cramped up.

I tried not to show it. I wanted to finish my breakfast. I'm sure pain crossed my face.

"What's wrong?" That's my mom leaping to the defense.

"Just feel like I have to burp," I said.

"No. You look worse than that. Is it the eggs? Have you developed an allergy?"

I shook my head.

"For Christ's sake, leave the girl alone. She said it's nothing," my dad said, rather annoyed. My mother's constant worry and obsession over death by living gets to him sometimes.

"This is our daughter!" Mom clearly wasn't going to back down, but Dad's interference was giving me enough time to pretend like it was just a little fluke.

"And I wish you'd let her live her life like she wants," Dad snapped.

Oh yeah.

Pink clouds of wish juice on their way. I felt myself smiling. Because that was like the best wish ever.

Suddenly I no longer felt the need to go running to the pool. Free at last!

Back upstairs, I danced around my room. I heard Eric start to get up, earlier than anyone expected after a late night. I felt bad for a moment that my jumping around might have woken him, but I didn't let it bother me for more than a second.

Finally! I was free! My mom would have to let me live the life I wanted. And I wanted so many things! I couldn't wait to see her face when I wanted to go off and have junk food.

The implications of what this wish could mean were huge. It was gonna be so great.

The down side was that I couldn't really gloat about it, because, you know. Wish talk. Can't happen.

It was going to be a royal pain to get Sage to believe that my mom just suddenly up and decided to listen to my dad about my life, but hey, those were details. This was the big picture. Me. My life. Like. I. Wanted.

I went back to dancing.

I texted with some friends. The weather was clear but no one was up to doing anything interesting. We'd just spent an evening together watching movies and a day inside. We talked about the mall, but although the roads were clear and the sky was as sunny as could be, not a cloud in sight, Ashley said her mom didn't want to let her go to the mall.

Lauren suggested the pool, but no one was all that excited about the pool, least of all me. Instead we just had a good text-versation. I listened to music on my bed. I had no doubt Lauren was studying something on her computer between texts.

If you think my mom has issues, Lauren's mom totally has issues, always pushing her to be better and do better. I mean my mom may not think I do anything right, but Lauren's mom is a slave driver, which meant Lauren had to at least look like she was studying something and not just playing on her phone.

Still, our conversation was all good, and when it got late and I was going to bed, I felt like Sunday had been a really good day which lulled me into a false sense of security about Monday.

Chapter Twelve

Bad wishes make you feel bad. — *The Fairy Godmother Handbook*

When I woke up on Monday, I was already feeling a little wish pressure. It felt pretty normal, so I thought I could probably hold onto it for a few hours. In fact, it was so low key that I could have been sitting next to someone who said, "I wish" right then and there and not automatically granted the wish.

I heard my mom downstairs running the vacuum cleaner. The air conditioner was on humming away. My brother was moving around, which meant he had to work.

I rolled over, getting tangled in the blankets that were just heavy enough to keep me from freezing when the air started to blow. It's not that we keep our house super cool, heaven forbid, but my mom worries that if it's too warm at night we won't sleep. It's set to let the house get warm in another hour or so. We had it set to start warming it up earlier, but Mom believes that if we cool the house down early on, then it stays cooler longer later on. Whatever.

Still, even with the wish pressure, I was feeling good.

Feeling free, I guess. Less worried. Because I only had one more day to get through before I went to the fairy godmother meeting. Then maybe I'd learn something more about the wishes. Heck, there were enough of us, if we had to, we could call a senior to explain things.

I remembered my interview and that made me get up quickly. I had to eat something and dress and see if my mom would let me take the car. We'd talked about it last week, but she could have forgotten. I pulled out a nice sundress and put on some closed-toe sandals instead of flip flops. I could put a sweater over the dress before I left.

"I've set up a schedule," my mom said as I came into the kitchen.

"A schedule?" I echoed, pulling out my usual yogurt and fruit.

"Yes. You'll do your laundry on Mondays. If you have cooking to do, you'll do that on Tuesday. You can clean your room any time, but you can't use the vacuum on Monday, Wednesday, or Friday mornings."

"OK?" I was wondering where she was going with this.

"Your father wants you to live your own life. Well, I'm going to help you. You can eat with us because we're family, and cooking for people is something I enjoy…"

I bit my tongue to keep from interrupting her to say she enjoyed telling us all what to eat.

"But from now on, part of you living your own life is doing your own laundry. I won't be coming into your room to clean anything, not even a light dusting any longer. If you run out of underwear it will be your own fault."

I nodded. I did my own laundry from time to time, like when I had a favorite outfit I wanted to wear again. It wasn't something I had to do every week, but how hard could it be? Also, I did clean my room. Yes, my mom dusted and vacuumed, but again, how hard could that be?

My mom gave me a long look. "Once Eric goes back to college, you'll be in charge of cleaning up your own bathroom, too. I won't make you clean up after him—although when he's home for short breaks and long weekends, you get to negotiate with him about what he needs to do to keep things clean."

She turned and left the room before my jaw hit my chest.

I was supposed to be living my own life, not cleaning up after my brother.

I tried to think of something to say. Something pithy. Something short. Something to get her attention about how that wasn't fair. Eric was living his own life, and he wasn't saddled with cleaning the bathroom. And he probably wouldn't be. Like I've said before, my mom can be so sexist!

I stomped around the kitchen and slammed the refrigerator door as I put things away. I mean, was she going to decide I had to do my own dishes whenever I ate something with the family, while she cleaned up after everyone else? It was like I was becoming a slave in my own house!

I ruminated on that while I ate. In fact, I was so mad, I didn't even taste the berries in my breakfast and I couldn't tell you if they were blueberries or raspberries.

I went and rinsed my dish and left it in the sink. Then I went upstairs. I was still mad. Didn't she know that we shouldn't eat when we're mad? That it's bad for the digestion or something? In fact, didn't I learn that fact from her?

I slammed the door to my bedroom and decided to get on the computer. I was mad enough that I didn't care that I had a wish building. I didn't care that I would probably just grant the first "I wish" I heard.

Because if it messed up the world, it was my mom's fault.

Because she was being horrible and petty about this whole 'let Willow live her life' thing.

I mean only my mother could have messed up a really excellent wish like the one my dad made.

Which meant, of course, that the wish showed up when I wasn't paying attention. The really, icky, horrible, I-should-never-have-granted-that wish that came about because I wasn't paying attention.

I've granted bad wishes before, but that was more because I didn't understand what I was doing. This time I knew better.

"I wish no one ever had to die."

I popped in and saw a little girl in a hospital, and she was sweet as can be, that sort of Southern girl, all blonde-haired and blue eyes and round-faced. She was probably five or six, and she was being held by her dad, who looked wrecked, with shadows under his eyes. They were pacing in a hallway painted white and that hospital-puke green. The antiseptic smell was overwhelming.

My pink cloud flowed out to her before it hit me what she'd said. I was sitting in a chair in a lounge across from where they paced looking at closed doors. I was in a corner, so no one probably noticed me. No one ever notices the pink cloud, either. It swirled around her, and I swear it made a face at me. Then I felt like I was going to puke.

I mean, I've granted bad wishes before, and they don't feel good. I even granted one that sort of created an alternative universe or something. That had felt icky, but not like this.

I barely made it out of the hospital and back to my

room. I ran out of there and got to the toilet in time to let loose. It was bad.

I was so never eating yogurt again. And it was blueberries this morning. Blueberries.

"Willow?" My mom knocked on the partially-closed bathroom door. I'd been in too much of a rush to close it all the way.

I felt more stomach bile coming out as I emptied everything in it. Man, this was clearly a very bad wish. If it worked like the last one, I might be able to reverse it, if I found a senior or a full-blooded fairy godmother. But I would have to do that before I granted another wish or this one would become permanent. And who knows if reversing it would even work. I mean, sun spots, right?

"Are you okay?" Now Mom had pushed the door open and was in the bathroom with me, standing over me as breakfast, or maybe it was the remnants of last night's dinner, came up and out.

"Is it nerves about the job interview? If you don't get this one, you'll find something else," my mom said.

I rested my cheek on the cool side of the toilet. At least I didn't have the pool compulsion on me.

Can you imagine? Puking at the pool? Ugh. I'd have probably gotten banned from the pool forever, and with the wish compulsion, I'd have probably tried sneaking in, over the fence even, just to be there. It would have been horrible.

"If you're sick, let me call them and tell them," my mom insisted

I'd have answered but, well, you know. Hard to talk when your stomach was trying to force its way up through your throat, because that's what it felt like.

I heard my phone ding like I had a text, probably from Sage. I wanted to get it, but as soon as I moved, the sour smell of old food overwhelmed me and I was back to the bowl.

"Let me get you something for that. I'm sure I have ginger tea," my mom said. "Then go to your room and lie down. If it doesn't stop, we'll call the doctor."

Like I needed a doctor. A doctor wasn't going to help. This was like epic bad. In fact it was probably the most epically bad wish ever.

And thanks to it, I was going to miss the interview. Of course, I probably wasn't in any condition to interview in a grocery store. I watched my car dream float a little further out of reach. Just when everything was coming together!

My mom left and I finished what I was doing. I was able to get up and rinse my mouth a bit and flush. That helped the smell.

I slipped back down against the sink and looked at the white porcelain of the toilet and the tub that sat next to it. Have you ever really looked at a bathroom? I mean our floor tile was blue gray with grayer grout between the tiles. They were large tiles, set so they looked like diamonds. I used to trace the patterns when waiting for the tub to fill, back before my mom decided I used too much water taking baths and I had to shower.

I leaned back wondering if I would still have to take five minute showers, rather than luxuriating in the water as long as I wanted. My life, right? Of course, she still paid the water bill, so she could argue with me there. I sighed.

But the sigh let me know that the vomiting was done. I went back to my room and about jumped out of my skin to see someone standing in there.

Chapter Thirteen

---

*Certain infractions of the handbook rules and laws will result in the
person being banned from granting wishes*
— The Fairy Godmother's Handbook

"Well, you win the prize." Brin stood with her
hands on her hips beside my bed. Brin is what
they call a senior fairy godmother, meaning she's been a
fairy godmother for more than five hundred years. I met
her once before. She looks about eighteen or so with an
oval face and straight dark hair.

Today she was in low ride jeans and a crop top that
showed off a fairly flat belly. In fact, that's about what she
was wearing the last time, although I think her top was a
little longer. She looked pretty impressive when you
consider she's over five hundred years old. There were
hardly any lines on her face, but there was something in
her eyes that suggested that although she looked close to
my age, she was way older.

I groaned before turning around to close the door. "My

mom will probably be up with ginger tea soon enough," I said.

Brin cocked her head to acknowledge what I said before asking, "Even with sun spots, how on earth did you manage to grant that wish?"

"It just happened. I wasn't paying attention. I thought I had more time before I'd need to grant a wish. And I was mad at my mom... it just kind of popped out."

"We even warned you all that you had to be careful for the next few weeks." Brin raised her hands like she wanted to shake the sky.

"I've been doing my best. I've been trying to avoid doing anything horrible. I did accidentally grant my mom's wish that I'd go to the pool more often and I probably still have prune lines on my hands, but do you see me complaining? I granted someone's wish to buy a house. I had to look for that one, okay? But I looked. I can't help it that I wake up with wish power trying to push out."

Brin nodded. "I have to admit that, other than your freak storm, you've done pretty good compared to some. Paula burned down half of California last night. It's still burning, but a few of the full-bloods have contained it. We're not even trying to reverse things in most cases, because that's likely to make it worse."

"But you can't mitigate what I granted," I said. "It *has* to be reversed."

"There are already people who should have died, who are in pain, wishing to die," Brin said. "There are full-bloods out there granting those wishes. One of those people just has to phrase it well enough to make this a general reversal."

"So why are you here, then?" I asked.

Brin sighed. "You've come to the attention of the full

bloods once before. You wouldn't have, but you didn't like a wish you'd granted. So they want someone to monitor your wish granting to see if you can stay a fairy godmother."

"But that's not fair!" First my mom and now the full-bloods.

"They don't have to be fair," Brin said. "This one did kind of piss them off, though. In your favor is the fact that everyone is messing up and wishes are going wrong. There's even a pool among the seniors in my pod to see how long the spotlight stays on you before it moves to someone else."

That didn't make me feel better. I mean yeah, someone else would get the spotlight, but that didn't really mean that I wasn't going to be staying a fairy godmother, right?

"Isn't there something I can do?" I asked.

"Well, seeing you don't have any wish power going on at the moment, I suggest you have a nice afternoon. I'll see you at the meeting tonight. Because I get to join you in senior center hell."

Then she popped out. Like actually *popped*. There was even a little sound. She had to have done that on purpose.

I flopped down on my bed. Now I was really upset. I mean, just a couple of days ago I was thinking I wanted to give up this whole fairy godmother thing because it was so hard sometimes, but that would have been my choice. Now there were people threatening to take this wish stuff away from me. I didn't want that. It wasn't fair.

I mostly liked being a fairy godmother. It made me special.

My mom chose that moment to come with ginger tea. Now, I hate ginger tea, but I took it and thanked her.

"Your color looks a little high. I think you should stay in bed today."

"I can go to the interview. I still have time to make it," I said. "If you didn't call them already?"

"No... but I really think..."

I didn't let her finish. "I can do that and then come straight home and do laundry," I said, standing up.

"I'll do your laundry this week. I don't need you over-doing it if you're sick. I'll make some soup for lunch."

I nodded at her. I took the tiniest possible sip of the tea before I stood up to get ready to go, found my white sweater, and left the house. My mom had given me the car keys without comment.

"Be yourself. You'll do fine," she said as I walked out the door. "And remember! *It's a Whole New World!*" That song was, like, her mantra whenever something was going to change. Now I'd have to go an interview with a Disney movie song stuck in my head. Worse, I'd be hearing my mom sing it, and my mom is no one's idea of the next American Idol.

At any rate, I got to the store on time, and met with the nice assistant manager, Nancy, a young woman not much older than I was. She had very black hair and three silver earrings in her ears. I thought I saw a dot on the side of her nose, like she'd had a nose ring, but either she'd gotten tired of it or they didn't let her wear it at the store. Probably the latter. I mean that's the whole reason my mom wouldn't let me get a nose ring.

"You could ruin your chances for a good job in the future, Willow," my mom had said when I asked about getting one.

No amount of arguing would get her to change her mind. Well, look at this. This girl had had a nose ring, and she just took it out—and she was the one interviewing me about a job. Not that I really wanted to spend the rest of my life working in a grocery store or anything.

Nancy and I sat in this little cafeteria area next to the store's coffee shop. It looks out at the parking lot and all the tables are tiny black things. I kept my hands in my lap while she took notes on a form about my answers.

The interview went well, I thought. Nancy said they would call me the next day to let me know what they decided. If I made it through this round, there was one more round where I got to meet the store manager and a couple of the senior cashiers. She smiled like she thought I had a good chance, so I thanked her for her time and headed home.

It might have been good that I wasn't feeling that great because it meant I hadn't made any sarcastic comments to her questions. I mean she asked me what I saw myself doing in five years. Like she expected me to say "working in a grocery store"?

I suppose, if I stayed working at the store, I could have a nose ring.

When I got home, my mom was in the kitchen chopping vegetables to add to the homemade chicken bone broth she was starting to heat. Lunch would likely be in about an hour.

"How did it go?" she asked.

"Pretty good, I guess. They said they'd call me for a second interview tomorrow, if I was one of their top choices."

My mom nodded. "That's good. At least there's a time-line, so you aren't waiting half the summer to hear back. Are you sure you need to work? You could just save your allowance for a car, you know."

Yeah. Like the allowance I got had any room for saving. I shook my head.

After lunch, I was kind of restless, and I was feeling bummed about the whole "you might be banned from being a fairy godmother" thing. I mean, this was so not my fault, so why was I being blamed? I went up to my room and laid on my bed. I felt tears leaking from my eyes. I hadn't realized I liked being a fairy godmother that much.

The day passed and then we had dinner and I came back upstairs to wait for seven o'clock, when I normally get transported to the meeting room. Seven came and went, and I was still in my room. Had they decided already? Had I really been banned?

Chapter Fourteen

Wish granters have very little control about the need to grant a wish
— The Fairy Godmother Handbook

J ust as I was going to try and focus on the room to see if I could get myself there, Brin popped in.

"No one is getting the pull, so I'm having to get you all for the meeting," she said. "Hold my hand."

I grabbed it. Suddenly I was falling. My stomach didn't fall as fast as the rest of me, or at least that's how it felt. First my poor stomach had felt like it had been coming up through my throat when I'd been vomiting and now I was losing it while traveling to the meeting. If this kept up, I was going to need a wish of my own to keep my poor stomach in place.

Finally I landed in the basement. Brin wasted no time letting go and going off to get someone else. Sergei and Connie were already there.

"It is bad that we can't even transport here," Sergei said.

"Has this happened before?" I asked. "I mean the sun spots?"

Connie shook her head. "Not to my knowledge. I tried reading the manual last Tuesday, to see if they'd added information about sun spots, but I didn't find anything. I think what's happening is different."

"It's not good," Sergei said. "I turned an entire city into Hello Kitty people, because I granted a wish for a little girl who said she wanted to see more of Hello Kitty. It should have been a safe wish."

"So that was you!" I exclaimed.

Sergei and Connie looked blank.

"I granted a wish for someone who wanted cooler weather, and it turned into a major snow storm. I decided to see if anyone else was having issues. The pink people were in the news. They didn't talk much about Hello Kitty, though."

Sergei looked both pleased and embarrassed that he had made the news.

Brin popped in with Grace. Moments later she had Brian. Finally she brought Deliza and Jesus.

We compared notes. Grace had granted a wish to a woman that her cat was healed of its cancer, and it had shrunk to kitten size and started playing like a young thing. Brian had granted a wish for a guy to make a million dollars. A few days later he found out the guy had been arrested for passing large amounts of counterfeit money.

After a few minutes Brin popped in with Cole, Sue, and Paula, so we were all there.

"So this isn't an ordinary meeting," Brin said. "Things are worse than the full-bloods thought they would be. Is everyone granting daily wishes?"

There were nods all around.

Brin nodded. "So have I. So far as we can tell just about everyone is. There have also been some rather bad wishes granted. Willow granted a wish to a little girl that people wouldn't die. The full-bloods are listening for an appropriate wish to undo that one. Here's the thing. We're finding that wishes that normally wouldn't be granted, like Willow's, *are* being granted. Plus, things can't be rectified as easily."

Sergei drew in a breath as if he wanted to ask a question. Brin held up a hand.

"To that end, I want you to think of me, and wish for me to come to you, if you believe you've granted a bad wish so we can look for someone to undo the wish or listen for a voice to wish for the opposite."

"And no," Brin said looking over at Sergei, "We can't undo the pink faces unless someone wishes they all *didn't* look like Hello Kitty anymore, and no one has. Individuals have, but they haven't used words that would allow the wish to encompass everyone who was affected."

"Can I wish for that?" Sergei asked.

"I don't have a wish to grant today. Mine are coming, like so many, at the early hours of the morning."

Again nods. So it wasn't just me.

"The full-bloods say they've only seen something like this once before, about nine-hundred years ago, which is before my time," Brin said. "They've been talking about how bad it is."

Grace nodded at that, her face flaming. Right now, her little kerfuffle with the dead husband's body was sounding pretty minor to me. Of course, she might have granted another wish that the rest of didn't know about. I wondered what would make her so embarrassed.

"What can we expect?" Connie asked. She picked off some cat fur from her dress.

"It will get worse through Wednesday, but then things

should drop off. Be very careful about your next wishes," Brin said. "Everyone." She looked at me like I was to blame.

Come on. If everyone was that bad off, why was I being singled out?

"We just think of you and call you?" Connie asked.

"Wish for me." Brin said. "It won't be a wish that gets granted, but I'll hear it because you have my name, my face, and your intention, as well as the word 'wish'. If I don't come right away, I'm helping someone else. You aren't the first group I've had to talk to, although I'll be closer to this one because I'm supposed to monitor Willow."

I made a face when she said that. I was the one getting monitored. Everyone was making bad wishes, and I was getting monitored. That so sucked.

We talked some more about strategies to keep from granting bad wishes. When it came to me, I mentioned listening to a lot of music until the wish pressure got so huge that I had to find someone wishing. There were nods all around. Even the people who hadn't been listening to loudly pounding music, had been working on their meditation.

"It's clear we can't just meditate this away," Brin said. "We have to think of something else."

"Valium?" Sergei asked. "You know, in large doses? So we sleep?"

Paula nodded as if she were thinking about it. "But would the wish pressure get large enough to wake us up, even out of that?"

"We could try knocking someone over the head and putting them out, and see if that works," Brian suggested. "You know, put someone into unconsciousness."

Great. Now they were thinking about scrambling my brain?

"Another group tried that," Brin announced. "The person woke up when the wish pressure got the greatest. About noon, I think. Then he went back into unconsciousness. When he woke the second time, just because he was coming out of it, he didn't even remember he'd granted a wish."

Just what I'd need now. I'd probably grant something even worse than 'no death' while I was unconscious, and the full-bloods would decide it was my fault. I was feeling rather pissed at Ashley, because it was her wish I'd accidentally granted that had gotten me noticed in the first place. If she hadn't wished her brother didn't exist, I probably wouldn't have gotten in quite so much trouble for granting the 'no death' wish.

"So we can't sleep through the sun spots or remain unconscious," Paula ticked off the lists. "Has anyone found anything that works?"

Brin shook her head. "Not that I know of. Someone barricaded themselves in their house and watched movies all day, but they popped out when the wish pressure got too strong."

That sounded like fun. Too bad my mom would never have gone for that.

I had tried wishing for myself, but hadn't been able to grant a wish. But after listening to them all, I *did* have an idea that just might work. I wasn't going to say anything yet because I really didn't want more attention on me. If it worked, it would totally keep me out of more trouble, which was exactly what I wanted.

Chapter Fifteen

Senior fairy godmothers are often set specific tasks, like monitoring
newer godmothers — The Fairy Godmother Handbook

Though the meeting threatened to drag on forever, it
finally finished. Fortunately, I was able to pop home
without Brin taking me there. I mean I literally _popped_
home. I love that. It often makes me wonder what would
happen if I were out and about, and then I popped out
and back in and how that would work. I mean, would
people even notice? Because it seems like everything is set
up so that we don't get noticed when we grant wishes
and stuff.

Monday at seven every single frigging week? You
cannot tell me that someone didn't mess up. Or didn't have
to be in the hospital, or something.

"It happens," Brin said. She'd clearly popped in to my
room while I was looking at the door. Now, she was sitting
on my bed in her low rise jeans, looking through one of my
fashion magazines, like she'd been there forever.

"Can you read minds?" I asked. I think I'd asked her before but she hadn't said.

"Only yours."

"Why? Because you have to watch me?"

"Because you're a teenager," Brin said. There was something dry in her voice that made me think she was making fun of me. I'd seen her work before and I totally didn't believe her.

I had to push it. "Will I outgrow it?"

"From the way your mother reacts to things, probably not." Brin didn't even bother to look up.

I heard my brother walk past my door. He had a grilled cheese—I could smell it from here. It made my stomach growl, even though I'd eaten earlier.

"Your whole family is surprisingly expressive, if you know what to look for."

"And you do?" I totally thought she was lying. I bet she could read anyone she wanted to. It was probably some super-secret senior-fairy-godmother power or something.

Brin shrugged.

"Do you, like, play poker, too?" My dad always talked about poker faces.

"I used to. It was easier when no one expected women to have a brain. There are times when progress and respect just don't pay." She looked up at me this time, smiling.

I thought about what she'd said, wondering what that must have been like. I mean, think of it. If you knew you could beat anyone at all, because you could read minds. That would be awesome. Except when it wasn't. I mean, would I really want to know what my brother thought about?

"Besides, gamblers make wishes all the time, mostly small," Brin said.

I wondered if I could pop into Las Vegas and grant a

few wishes for poker players to win a game. Did they play during the day, or did they just play at night in smoke-filled rooms?

Brin shook her head. "People gamble all the time. There are casinos everywhere, but you need to focus on tuning into them."

"Why didn't you suggest that to everyone?" I asked.

"I suggested it a few nights ago. One casino had to close, because there was such a run on its resources. Someone granted a wish that sounded like a wish to win a jackpot, and it was fulfilled in a way that nearly ruined the casino."

"Man, this sun spot thing sucks."

"You think you've got it bad?" Brin asked, looking at me over the top of the magazine. I slumped down at the foot of my bed.

"Who has it worse? I'm being watched for something I can't control any more than anyone else can."

"I'm the one who has to watch you," Brin said.

"It's not like you'll lose your ability to grant wishes if you fail. This is stressful." I laid back down. "It's not like I thought that no death was a good thing, really."

"I could be home," Brin said. "Instead I'm here. And when I'm not here, I have to listen. I'll probably be popping in and out to go solve problems all over the world. You don't think that's tiring? Plus, I have to control my own wish-granting."

I looked over at her. She was glaring at me as if my worries were petty. Tough biscuits if they were. They were my worries. I wasn't, like, five hundred years old with my own place. I had crap to work out.

I mean, even though I wasn't having to run to the pool every single day, I still had to apply for a job so I could get a car. I bet Brin had a really fancy car.

I got up and found my music player and laid back down listening to it. If Brin weren't there, I might have danced or messed on the computer, but with her just sitting on my bed watching everything I did, there was no way. Even if she was looking at a magazine. It was too weird.

I wanted to lean against my pillows, but Brin was doing that. In fact, it was starting to annoy me that she had to be in my room with me. What was up with that? Did she think watching me every minute of every day, when she had said she knew that most wish power came up in the morning, was really going to help?

"At some point, you know, I'm going to want to go to bed," I said, looking at her. I raised one of the earbuds from my ears so I could hear if she answered.

"I know." She flipped a page in the magazine and kept reading.

I sighed. If only someone had wished that there would be regular death, or something like that, and I could get my life back. I got tired of listening to music and texted Sage on my phone.

Ashley and Lauren got in on the action and we had a nice conversation, if that's what you call something that's all in writing. I banged my legs against the bed so that it moved. Brin didn't appear to notice. She was very good at being oblivious. Still, I kept at it.

I mean what could a five hundred year-old want with a fashion magazine? Did she really need to keep up on styles?

"Actually," Brin said, "I spent some time as a dress-maker, so yes, I do like to keep up on styles."

I glared. She wasn't supposed to read my mind.

Brin smiled.

"How long were you a dressmaker?" I asked finally.

"Just about a decade. Then I had to leave. The whole

slow aging thing can be problematic. Stay in one place too long and people think you're a witch or a vampire or some other sort of demon and they hate that," Brin said, looking up from the magazine.

"Did that ever happen to you?" I mean, people didn't believe in that stuff now, so would I have to worry as much?

"It's happened to all of us at one time or another. And just because they don't really believe in that stuff now, don't think the modern age doesn't have its drawbacks. A hundred years ago, I could just move a few miles away and no one would know me. Now? Now you have the internet."

Where everyone would see you didn't age.

"So what do you do now?" I asked.

"It hasn't gone on long enough to be a problem yet," Brin said. "We're still working on it. It probably won't take as long to figure out as it did for us to get the handbook online, though."

We talked a bit more and then I went and changed into my pajamas. I wear a nightshirt with shorts. It's not a full nightshirt, as it only comes down to my hips, and it matches the shorts. They're all black with stars and planets and crap on it. It's better than kittens or puppies, which I *so* would *not* wear.

I came back out and looked at Brin. "Can I go to sleep now?"

"I don't know," she said. "Can you?" She did set aside the magazine which was a hopeful sign.

"You're on my bed." I stood there, looking at her, from the foot of the bed.

"So?"

"So?" I said back. I was ready to start yelling at her.

How did she expect me to sleep if she was sitting right where I would lay down if I went to sleep?

Brin gave me a smile. "You're so worried about me staying here all night. I am supposed to watch you, but I can sleep elsewhere." With that she popped out. Like if I had gotten mad at her earlier she might have left sooner?

I rolled my eyes. Save me from senior fairy godmothers and full-bloods and anything else with power like that, because they were more than a little annoying. Maybe it's the whole power thing. They know they have it and they use it, just not always for good.

I crawled under the covers and tossed and turned for a long time. I was mad at Brin. I was worried about the next day. I was pissed off that no one had bothered to wish that death would come along just like normal.

"I wish," I said, deliberately, knowing I was being listened to. "That people would be able to die like they all used to, just normally."

A sort of cold fog gathered around me, reaching up inside me. I thought I saw the faintest edges of silver blue. I hoped it was someone granting my wish. I also hoped that I hadn't made the wrong wish, one that would make things worse. Well at least I wasn't the one granting it.

Chapter Sixteen

When sunspots happen, any fairy godmothers who grant a bad wish
will recite the opposite of that wish until the problem is fixed.
—*The Revised Fairy Godmother Handbook*

Tuesday morning came. The wish pressure sat in my belly bigger than ever. If granting a normal wish was like giving birth, this felt like I was carrying triplets. Or maybe even more. In fact, if I were a dog, I'd be having a litter. It *so* did not feel good. In fact, I'm not sure I'll ever look at dogs the same again. I have no idea how they do it.

My clothes still fit when I dressed, and honestly, it sort of surprised me.

I didn't have an appetite. It was like I knew I couldn't fit anything more into my body. My mom would have a fit if I didn't go downstairs, though.

I brought my phone and used it to play some music while I puttered around the kitchen. I could use the excuse that I was waiting for a call back about that job. I pulled out a bowl, but I didn't put anything in it. I sat with it and then put it in the sink. While I rinsed it out, I wondered where my mom was. I finally saw the note that said she had an acupuncture appointment and would be back later.

I sighed. Great. I'd hoped that I could talk to her about what I wished, and then she'd echo me and say what she wished, and it would be something little and innocuous. But no, she had to be off to the acupuncturist.

This so did not bode well. I felt like crap. If she knew that, she'd send me there, too. And what? I'd pop out with needles stuck in me like some teenage voodoo doll?

Now, I like Mom's acupuncturist. She's treated me for some colds and things like that and helped heal my wrist when I fell off the top of the car—long story. I just didn't want to be trapped on a table with needles stuck all over and be fighting the wish pressure.

I felt even heavier going up the stairs. In fact, I felt so weighted down that I worried I was going to fall through the floor

I was hearing wishes, but they all seemed big wishes.

"I wish my mom wouldn't die." So not touching that one.

"I wish the world was a more peaceful place." Tempting, because how bad could it be? But not touching it, not today. The wish might just destroy all humans—and then where would I be? Out of a job, that's for sure.

"I wish it were cooler." Yeah. Been there. Done that.

"I wish it weren't raining."

"I wish I could go to the park." Bingo.

I floated myself there, to a rich-looking house with a little boy in shorts, looking out a window. I landed on the sidewalk across the way, under a large shade tree. The old brick houses were two stories tall, mostly, and what my mother would call stately. A rich neighborhood that had been rich for a hundred years. Cars passed a few blocks away, but this street was quiet. The sidewalks were raised here and there from tree roots that had gotten too big.

I blew out my breath, releasing the wish, sending my usual pink cloud to him.

I nearly toppled over when the land moved. Like an earthquake. I held onto the tree so tightly I smelled the sap inside the trunk. I could have popped out, but I held out against that. I wanted to know what was happening.

Then *plop*. In the middle of the street was a play park. Apparently this kid wasn't going to have to go far to get to the park.

I popped out. "Jesus H. Christ," I swore when I was back in my room.

"You said it," Brin said, waiting in my room.

"I thought I'd changed my wish?" I said. "I felt it— someone granted it. Death is back. So what are you doing here?"

"So you did, thank heavens. If we'd thought about it, we'd have had you reciting that as a mantra. In fact, it's probably being noted now. Just have all fairy godmothers recite mantras of wishes that need to be granted to undo other wishes," Brin said. "But that doesn't mean I'm not still watching. I just have to watch someone else who wished an end to the drought in Africa, and now every-thing is flooding. It's also likely to cause problems in Europe if we don't move the weather patterns back to where they were before."

"But the park in the middle of the street?" I asked.

Brin shrugged. "No one could have seen that coming. It seemed like a safe enough wish to me."

I rolled my eyes and sat back on my bed. "This sucks."

"I know."

"I wish the sun spots would go away," I said.

"Everyone has tried that wish. It doesn't work," Brin said drily.

I gave her a long look. I should have thought of that ages ago.

"I wasn't even thinking," I muttered.

"Oh I know. Even if you had been, it wouldn't have worked. Several have tried. We've even managed to manipulate people into wishing that. Sort of like I bet you hoped to do with your mom. The chances of it working are iffy. It has to be something they'd want anyway."

"Well I really want the sun spots to go away," I said looking at her.

I felt another wish starting to press on me.

"Crap."

Brin looked at me. She sighed. "This could get bad for a couple of days. Hold onto that one as long as you can, okay? I have some other trouble spots to take care of."

She popped out.

I grabbed my MP3 and started listening to music. It was the best way I knew to avoid granting a wish until I was ready.

Unfortunately, no matter what tune I went to, I kept hearing "I wish." I knew that's not what the words were, but that's what my mind was making them be.

I so did not like this. The sun spots were getting worse, and they'd been bad enough before. At least I wasn't on the top of the watch list any longer. Even so, I couldn't afford to get annoyed and grant a wish I'd regret.

I wanted to wish that this was over, but that might mean "all life" or maybe *my* life if someone granted it. Look what happened to the blasted park. It's like the sun spots wanted the wishes to go wrong.

That kid better appreciate getting his own park after

that wish. Of course, his parents were probably pretty pissed. It looked like the park blocked their driveway.

I was bouncing around on the bed to music, trying to keep my mind off of wishes, when the door opened. My mom stood there looking at me.

"What?" I raised an earbud.

"Just checking on you," she said.

"I'm fine."

My mom *humphed* and left. I put the earbud back in. I couldn't really blame her if she didn't believe me because it wasn't true. Normally I lie better than that, but this wish pressure was really bad and I was totally off my game.

My analogy towards having twins or triplets was apparently spot on, because this was my second wish of the day. Wishes were starting to flow through my head.

"I wish I was the president."

"I wish I was older." Tempting but probably bad.

"I wish I was younger." Same thing although the idea made me laugh so hard that I felt myself start to pop but I froze and started chanting something else. I caught it in time.

"I wish I could win."

I had no idea what they wanted to win, but it reminded me of Brin's casino story. While she said there were casinos everywhere, the only ones I knew of were in Las Vegas so I thought about it.

Pretty soon there was a ton of noise in my head, bells ringing and sirens going, music, old music really, playing too loudly. I smelled citrus and sweat and faint traces of cigarette smoke. Lights were everywhere. It was all sort of superimposed on my bedroom like I had half popped to Las Vegas. I listened more closely but no one was saying or even thinking, "I wish," which meant there was nothing I could do to help.

I closed my eyes because I was getting dizzy from that double-vision thing. Then *plop* I was just back in my room on my bed. My whole body felt really uncomfortable. In fact, I was almost dancing like I had to pee really badly.

"I wish I had hair." This would probably go wrong, but I zipped over there. An older woman was in a hospital and she was very sick. Her skin was pasty pale, like milky white. I was on the narrow ledge by her room looking in. Don't ask. It just happens. It's a weird thing about wish granting.

I almost didn't want to do it. Wishes were going bad, but how bad could this be? She wanted hair and she was pretty bald. So *poof.* I let the pink cloud go. And there she was. Bride of Chewbacca. She had hair everywhere, all over her body, long and brown and sort of silky.

I snickered at the window. She looked up, confused. I popped out before she could get a look at me.

When I got back to my room, Brin wasn't waiting for me, which was a good thing. At least no one was yelling at me for turning the woman into a Wookie. Heck, her grand-kids would probably love it.

I drew in a breath and then let it out, relieved. Two wishes down and one more day. I thought I was free for the rest of the day. Except I wasn't.

Chapter Seventeen

You will not be able to mention being a fairy godmother, even if you
desire to — The Fairy Godmother Handbook

I thought I was going to get to go on about my day.
Maybe even go to the mall with Sage so we could try
and entice Doug over to our table and she could flirt
some more.

But no. I was barely back to my room when the wish
pressure started mounting again.

I shook my head, not sure what else to do. I had a lot
of thoughts, and trying to express any of them would have
gotten me grounded for months.

I dropped back on my bed with the MP3. The music
beat was fast. I tried to lose myself in it, eyes closed, feeling
the softness of the bed behind me and smelling the clean
fresh scent of the sheets that up until now my mom had
always washed.

Was I going to have to do that myself, too?

My mom knocked again, then walked in. I sat up,
looking at her.

"That's it," she said. "You look pale. Are you sure you feel fine?"

"Pretty much," I said, wondering how I could look pale after all the time I'd spend at the pool last week, thanks to her.

I went to go back to listening to my music. I watched her leave.

She came back a few minutes later, hardly even half a song.

"I called the acupuncturist and we're going. Something is going on, even if you won't tell me. Maybe you'll tell Luci."

"What?" I asked.

My mom basically pulled me up out of the bed and frog-marched me down the hall and the stairs, forcing me to keep going. Fortunately, she didn't make me take off my earbuds. At least I'd have my music.

It made me wonder what would happen if I heard a wish and popped out with her there. I'd never been close to anyone when a wish came before. This was like what I was thinking about the other day, and now I might have to test it. Great, if I blew that, it would be one more strike against me from the fairy godmothers.

Up until now, I'd always managed to excuse myself to go to the bathroom, so no one would see me pop out and back in. I just had to flush and pretend it was nature calling. I guess that was sort of the truth—*something* was calling, just not Mother Nature.

In the car, I tried to avoid listening to the wish words I was hearing around me.

"I wish I had a better job." If I wasn't trapped in the car, I might have tried to grant that one.

"I wish I had bigger boobs." Really?

"I wish he hadn't left." No. So no. Not right now.

"I wish I weren't so fat." No. Bad enough to grant that one when there weren't sun spots. Another wish issue.

"I wish…" and you get the idea.

I tried to listen to my music, but my mom kept looking at me as if there was a problem.

"What?" I asked.

"I wish you'd tell me what's wrong."

I felt the wish power starting to release, but I clamped down on it as hard as I could. It was like trying to keep from peeing when you really, *really* had to go.

"Shit. I am so sick of traffic. I wish I could get through." I glanced out. It was the woman next to us in her car, looking irritated as we came to a stop at a light. I let the wish power flow through to her. I had no idea exactly what she meant, but it allowed me to grant a relatively minor wish without leaving the car.

I watched as the pink cloud dissipated. The woman looked up, then drove around the car in front of her, slipping through just as the light changed to red. She made it and continued down the shoulder of the street.

"I just can't believe people sometimes," my mom said mildly as the other car swerved and sped through the slower moving traffic.

I hoped the woman who made the wish didn't get killed. But at least I was wish free for the moment.

The moment lasted almost to the acupuncturist's, which is about fifteen minutes from my house. The length of time between when I started feeling wish pressure after I granted my last wish made me hope that they were coming less frequently.

I felt the next stirrings when I got out of the car in front of my acupuncturist's office. It's a long, low building, one of those in a square of small, commercial offices, and shares the parking lot with the dentist's office next door.

The door to Luci's office is maroon, and is next to a big window that looks into her reception area. She has a huge image of a mountain in the background, with a very small person about to climb it. There's no words on it, so it's not like some inspirational quote thing or anything, just a big picture. It's sort of inviting, along with the sofa and two chairs all in pale blue gray that sit in the waiting area.

The office has tile floors and in the waiting the floor is covered with one of those big blue rugs that have all the small printed flowers on them. The walls are done in cream. The place always smells a bit smoky-sweet and sort of musky from the herbs she mixes.

Luci wasn't in her place behind the counter, which meant she was with a patient, so my mom and I sat down to wait. My mom had her own phone, which she started fiddling with while I waited, quietly, not playing on my phone, just wondering how acupuncture was going to work with the wish pressure.

The music in the background was supposed to be soothing, a light flute kind of thing, but it wasn't soothing me at all, not that day. I tried to breathe. Luci was always telling me to breathe but this wasn't helping. In fact, it felt as if there was no room for air in my lungs. The wish pressure, that need, was too much.

My phone vibrated and I grabbed it before it made too much noise.

It was the interviewer, Nancy. They wanted me to come in tomorrow around three. I thanked her and hung up, giving my mom a very smug smile.

My mom, busy with her worry, just sighed.

I hoped Luci would hurry. I didn't know how long I could hold onto the wish pressure. Maybe I should run to the bathroom quickly and then get it over with.

"I wish he wasn't here." Oh no. Not granting that one.

"I wish I had that purse." And psst... gone. Too late. That would have been a great one to grant. Of course the way things were going, not seeing the person, but just hearing them, she might have been admiring someone else's purse and then who knows? She might have been arrested for purse snatching. I smiled a little at the thought.

"I wish I had a better job." Not granting it. Mom was sitting there, not really paying attention, but I didn't want to chance that by popping in and out.

Can you imagine the conversation?

"Willow, where did you go?"

Me. "Um... nowhere?"

Yeah. She'd buy that. Not.

I stood up to adjust my shorts, thinking about making a break for the bathroom. This wish pressure was just getting too much.

"Are you okay?" my mom said about the same time as Luci walked into the reception to take me back.

"Come on back, Willow," Luci said smiling.

She's tall and thin and pretty. Her hair hangs down to her shoulders and it's almost always pulled back. She laughs about everything, really. Sometimes I think she's closer to my age than my mom's.

I know she's an adult, a real adult. It's just that she acts like a kid sometimes. I wish my mom had as much fun as she did. In fact, given my mom's general personality, I'm surprised she goes there. Because health for my mom is *really* serious. And Luci is anything but.

We walked down a short, wide hallway and into a treatment room. There were more of those pictures that looked sort of Chinese, but weren't. The walls were all painted a sort of green, which was an odd color with the lights. Luci had bamboo sticks hanging from the ceiling and sheer fabric looped through them to cover the fluorescent lights and make it darker.

I climbed up on the table, which is like a regular, old massage table, according to my mom. Luci always has flannel sheets in light colors covering it, probably so she can bleach them. No blood. My mom is paranoid about someone else's blood even being in her vicinity. If she got any worse about her phobia, she probably wouldn't ever go out, because someone with blood flowing through their veins would stand next to her.

"So what's going on?" Luci asked, settling back on a tall wooden stool. It was high enough that she only sort of leaned back on it, but I had seen her climb up and sit as if we were going to have a conversation.

"Just not feeling quite right," I said. "It's not anything really. I think it will go away."

Luci waited, looking at me. She's got that sort of face, with wide eyes that make you want to tell her things. She never judges. I've told her a lot of things about me that I haven't ever planned to tell her. In fact, there was a part of me that wanted to tell her about the whole wish thing, but I found I couldn't even open my mouth when I considered that.

I shrugged as I got comfortable on the table. Luci went around adjusting the pillow beneath my head and making sure there was a bolster beneath my knees so I could lay there and be comfortable.

"But what's not quite right?" she asked.

If she only knew.

"I guess I feel a little bloated." That was honest enough.

"Well let's take care of that and get you feeling better again." Luci had me adjust my shirt so that she could reach my stomach. She started feeling around. Her pressing hurt and everything felt tender. It was like she was going to push the wish right out of me. I wondered where it would go if she succeeded.

"I don't feel anything," she said when she was done.

I had taken my shoes and socks off before getting on the table and she used a small alcohol wipe to clean the areas.

"My mom is just paranoid that something is going to happen and she'll miss it," I said.

"I wish more moms were like her," Luci said.

And *woop*. I tried to grab the pink cloud, hold it in physically—you know, the way people in slasher movies are always trying to hold their guts in? But it slipped right through my fingers.

I tried to drag back the wish. It felt like I was trying to catch a fish with my bare hands. It did give me hope, though, because I could feel myself almost grabbing onto something.

God what was I going to do if I had consigned millions of girls my age to mothers like mine? They'd all go crazy. Some might even kill their moms. Or, the way the wishes were going, they might all be at my house, thinking my mom was their mom. Oh good heavens, the things that could go wrong.

I reached out to physically grab the pink blob, hoping it wouldn't get to Luci. She turned in time to see me reaching. I don't know if she thought I was dusting something away or if she saw something, but she sort of brushed her hand around like she was clearing the air and the pink was gone.

Suddenly, I had wish pressure again. Was that how you rejected a wish? Just brush it away? I'd need to remember to suggest that at the meeting.

Luci started putting the needles in. I hated the way

they felt when they were in my stomach. I mean I don't normally mind, them but this seemed like it stirred up the wish pressure even more. I knew she'd leave as soon as the needles were in. I so didn't want to have to go out and grant a wish with needles but I was so uncomfortable.

"I wish I had new car." Still worried about the needles.

"I wish she liked me." Too much could go wrong.

"I wish he wasn't such an ass." Now there was something tempting but it passed before I could really fixate on it, which was a good thing.

"I wish there were more nice people in the world."

I liked that one and I let myself follow it. There was a homeless guy sitting on the ground with a hat in front of him. People were just walking by him, mostly not noticing, but he did have a dollar in the hat. I bet someone dropped it and he made his wish. I sent out the wish, my pink cloud flowing from my body and towards him.

That couldn't hurt anything, could it? At least not normally. Even if it did go wrong, how could anyone fault me for going after that wish?

I waited for a second, checking. Yep. Still had needles. Oddly, even though I was standing up and my top should have come down and covered them, the top was still hanging up around the upper part of my stomach. Weird.

I was already feeling a new bit of wish pressure. I hoped the homeless guy would make another wish, but he didn't.

A couple of people dropped coins in the hat while I was watching. He thanked them with a voice that was deeper than I expected.

I popped back to the treatment room, landing back on the treatment table, where I got to lay there, listening, while people vocalized their wishes. Sometimes it was just in passing, sometimes with more feeling. I was going to have to grant another one soon.

But the needles were in, and I was relaxing, and I finally did what I always do in an acupuncture treatment. I went to sleep.

Chapter Eighteen

Apparently some people only have a really bad need to grant a wish when they're in the sun. — The Collected Wisdom of Willow Vaughn

When Luci woke me up, the wish pressure was every bit as bad as it had been earlier. I was so going to need to grant a wish soon. But at least I hadn't popped out in front of my mom or something like that. That would have been bad. Even on the ride home, although I felt like a bloated cow, I made myself ignore wishes.

I had been given orders to drink water and to eat lightly. Well, I was probably going to do that anyway, because food did not sound appetizing. It was like the wish stuff was so big I didn't have room for anything else.

At least Luci telling me to eat lightly meant that if I didn't eat much, I wouldn't be freaking my mom out. I could tell her I was just doing as Luci asked, and she could be pleased that I was following my acupuncturist's recommendations.

I got back to the house and immediately headed for my

room. The wish pressure was heavy. It was like I had to go to the bathroom really, *really* badly. Now I understood why Brian compared it to a fart. No one was going to just push out a baby as easily as the wish could be pushed out, but it hurt more than any fart had ever hurt when you were trying to keep from granting a wish.

"Acupuncture?" Brin asked when I came in the room.

"I thought that wish was fixed," I said.

Brin shrugged. "Yeah, you did that. But I'm still supposed to watch you, along with six other people. As if I could be there with six people at once."

"You could wish for it," I said, glaring at her.

Brin glared back. "While I haven't been hit as hard as you—the wish pressure dissipates if I'm not in daylight—it's still there, so don't tempt me."

I was really tempting to say I wished this was over. My luck, it would kill me or I'd get banned from being a fairy godmother forever. So I kept my mouth shut.

"Did you notice what happened in the treatment room?" I asked.

Brin shook her head.

"My acupuncturist made a wish and I almost started to grant it. I tried to pull it back, but it was like trying to catch a fish with your bare hands…"

"You've done that?" Brin looked incredulous.

It took me a moment to realize she wasn't talking about pulling back a wish but about catching the fish in my bare hands.

"It's an expression? A metaphor?" Hadn't she had an English teacher drilling that crap into her when she grew up? Five hundred years old, though, probably not. Lucky her.

Brin just gave me a long stare. "Well, go on then…"

"It was like I could *almost* grab it back, but not quite.

My acupuncturist turned just as I was trying to grab it, and she waved her hand in front of her face like she was shooing away a fly, and the wish cloud disappeared—and suddenly I had to grant another wish really badly."

"So it was like she was thinking, go away, or something," Brin said.

I nodded.

"Interesting. But you know that doesn't help."

"Why not?" I mean this was a way to make sure wishes didn't get granted.

"The person wishing would have to know wishes were real. But they don't."

Well there was that. "What if we did that to each other?"

"We'd spend all day trying to do that? You said the wish seed came right back to you."

I sighed. "It seemed like something we could work with."

Brin nodded.

There was nothing to it but to try and lie down and look for a non-life threatening wish.

"I wish you the best of birthdays!" I heard the woman's voice in my head.

I popped out. There I was, in a graveyard, with a woman standing over the grave of what was obviously a child she'd lost. I sighed. Popped back out.

"You didn't grant that did you?" Brin asked when I popped back in.

"No. I was going to. It sounded safe."

Brin nodded. "Then you saw where she was. At least you're learning restraint and not granting practically as you pop through. We'll make a decent godmother of you yet."

I sighed.

I searched through the plethora of wishes.

"I wish I didn't have to go to summer school." I thought that should be safe. I popped out.

It was a boy about thirteen trudging down the street, head down. I wasn't sure if he was cutting class or if summer school hadn't started yet. He was wishing. So I sent off my pink cloud and it hit him in the back.

Wham. He no longer had to go to summer school.

I nearly screamed when I heard the squeal of brakes as a car turned the corner. It was going too fast. I could see the accident about to happen.

Chapter Nineteen

Fairy godmothers should leave as soon as the wish is granted — The Fairy Godmother's Handbook (revised)

I could feel myself becoming disoriented like I was going to pop out. I focused on the way the air felt on my skin, the smell of the trees, that sort of sappy, tangy scent that made my nose itch. I felt the hot pavement on my bare feet because I'm always barefoot at home. The sound of the engine revving high pushed me to move.

I ran across the street as fast as I could, pushing the boy out of the way. We fell into the soft grass of a yard and went rolling.

"What the…" he started to say as the car lost control and began to barrel towards us. The driver was paying enough attention and swerved around, hitting a telephone pole just ahead of where we lay.

The car's engine stopped.

"Wow…" the kid said. "How did you know?"

I shook my head, standing up. It felt like I was going to pop out any moment.

The kid was holding my hand. I drew my hand back.

With that I disappeared.

Great. There was going to be an article about the mysterious woman who saved the boy. The newspapers would make drawings, and people would look for me, and I'd have to explain to my mom what I was doing on that side of town in the middle of the day when I didn't feel good.

"No you won't," Brin said, a sneer in her voice. "But good job saving the kid."

"Well, you wouldn't think that's how a wish would go, would you?"

"Normally."

Yeah, normally.

"Well, normally I don't go around tackling the people I grant wishes to." I glared at her. She was back to lying across my bed.

"Do you remember what Carl looked like? Other than a creep?" Brin asked out of the blue.

Carl was the fairy godmother who had granted me the power to grant wishes. I didn't know that's what I was wishing for, but I wanted to wish for something that wasn't stupid and couldn't come back to haunt me. Failed on that second count.

At any rate, because he didn't want to be fairy godmother any longer, and I wished that I could make people happy—well sort of—I was mad at my mom because she's never happy. I never really thought about how he looked other than that he was creepy. Now that Brin asked, I realized, no, I couldn't have described him.

I tried. The harder I tried the more his looks eluded me.

Brin was watching me and not reading my mind like she always does, waiting for me to admit she was right.

"Okay. No. I can't."

She shrugged. "Neither will the kid. He'll remember you were a girl, but whether you were his age or his grandmother's, he won't be able to tell."

Thank heavens for small favors.

"Of course we don't know that the wish won't get granted in an equally evil way later on, but I suspect it will take the path of least resistance, which will be that someone will decide that he can't go walking along the street on his own because he might get hurt."

"What if the universe knew the whole time that I'd rescue him, and that was the plan?" I asked.

Brin gave me a long look. "Nothing is that predetermined. It's not like you stick around to save your wishees from themselves on a regular basis."

Not like I'd really want to. It would be way too sappy for me. I'd probably puke or something.

"Does anyone stand around? I sort of feel like I'm supposed to pop out."

"You are," Brin said. "Not doing so is sort of a violation, but this isn't normal, so they won't get mad at you for saving the kid."

Great. I was breaking rules I didn't even know existed.

"It's in the handbook—on page 203—if you read it."

"I have read it," I said. "I don't remember that rule."

I sat down at my computer and looked at the handbook. There were only 201 pages.

"There is no page 203." I turned to glare at Brin.

"Oops. Guess we haven't gotten the whole thing online yet."

I glared some more.

"Not my area," Brin said, holding her hands up.

Like that mattered at all.

Chapter Twenty

People really need to think through their wishes — Wisdom of Willow Vaughn.

The rest of the evening was uneventful. Brin popped out a couple of times. I didn't have another wish to fill, thank heavens. I was able to eat a normal dinner, although my mother insisted I not eat too much. She even served a cold pasta salad with chicken and too many vegetables. It smelled vinegary but tasted okay.

I liked the crunch of the vegetables and the cool feel on my tongue after the really warm day. Thank heavens I hadn't had to go to the pool, too. My dad and brother did most of the talking, which was a dry hum in the background as I concentrated on making sure my mom wasn't completely freaking out about how much or how little I was eating.

I left the table still hungry, but at least there wasn't a blob of wish pressure trying to get out. I was not looking forward to Wednesday, but I reminded myself that at least it was the last day of this thing. After that, stuff would start to get better. I hoped that my interview would be after the worst of it.

I texted with Sage and Lauren and Ashley. Lauren had some cheerleading camp thing that she was going to on the weekend, and that was all she was talking about. It almost made me wish I could be a cheerleader, but that just didn't suit my personality. I am so *not* a perky person.

Brin wasn't around when I crawled into bed. I wondered what she was up to, but not so much that I stayed awake wondering. I fell right to sleep. And woke at about five in the morning with this huge wish pressure. It was still dark out, so I listened for people wishing.

"I wish I didn't have to get up this early."

"I wish I didn't have to go to work today."

"I wish you'd let me sleep."

"I wish I didn't have a meeting."

All work-related stuff, and all pretty small.

I chose someone wishing they didn't have to get up that early at random, landed on an apartment balcony in downtown, and sent off my pink wish cloud. Who knew what it would do. But it was still mostly dark, the pink was just barely on the horizon, and I got rid of the wish pressure, or seed, as Brin called it.

Hopefully, with the sun not up fully, the wish wouldn't do anything horrible like burn down the building where they worked or something.

I turned over the idea of the wish seed. It was like a seed that grew and grew and started forcing its way up through my body, trying to get out. I pictured the monster from that movie *Alien*, screeching as it came out of me.

Except that didn't really happen. I mean, it was a cloud that no one but me, and probably other fairy godmothers, could see.

I was back in my room, curled under my covers, and

thinking about that while I drifted off. I woke perhaps an hour later, still earlier than normal, but this time there was more light in my room, and more wish pressure. At least this morning it seemed that they were coming one at a time and not all at once, like yesterday's wishes seemed to.

I hurried through the litany of wishes.

Someone was wishing they didn't have to go to work. I granted that. And wished, out loud, as I popped back home, "I wish that everyone around them is safe, and nothing bad happens to keep them from having to go to work today."

I even got a nice golden cloud around me, like someone was listening. I did a small happy dance before climbing back into bed and trying to get under the covers. I wondered if I could wish good things for all my wish granting to make sure people stayed safe?

I dozed off for a little while. I didn't sleep—sleep. I had too much wish pressure going on. You know when it's really early and you kind of have to pee, but you don't want to get out of bed? It was like that.

Anyway, I stayed in bed, trying to doze. I heard my mom get up and go downstairs. She really does walk like an elephant. My father tromped down shortly after her. He walks more like a horse.

Then Eric got up, which was really early for him. I wondered what his schedule was today. He made a ton of noise, like he was trying to wake me up. At least that would give me an excuse if I got up earlier than normal. It was full light now, which meant the sun spots were probably going to interfere in any wish I granted.

I sighed.

The pressure was growing.

"I wish I had a cherry tree." That got my attention. Who wishes for a cherry tree? Especially at first light.

"I wish I had a cow."

Are these wishes for real or was I not hearing right? If I wasn't hearing right then what were they really wishing for?

There were some normal wishes in there. "I wish I could sleep."

"I wish I had gotten more sleep."

"I wish I knew the ending." I wondered what show she wanted to know the ending to. If it were for something finished, like she was reading a book, then that wouldn't be bad, but if it was something else, well, that could create all sorts of messes.

"I wish he'd just leave."

Pop. Out I went. I didn't actually grant the wish though. I was in a run-down area and there were two women, one with dark hair, braided into thick, rich box braids that made my hands want to feel them, the other with her hair short and curled under, clearly molded within an inch of its life, talking by a bus stop.

I felt the pink cloud start to release but I held onto it. I didn't think the woman with the braids really wanted the man to just leave. She was outside just talking for heaven's sake. I didn't pop out back to my bedroom.

There weren't many people out in this area, but those that were, were all gathered around the stop. A few old cars drove down the street.

"Sometimes I wish he'd leave so you'd stop talking about him," her friend laughed.

I held onto the wish pressure like a lifeline. In fact, I leaned back. It was like playing tug of war.

"I wish someone else would wish," I muttered holding onto the wish.

"Man, I wish the bus would get here, so I don't have to listen to you two," some old guy said. I released the wish pressure. The bus turned the corner and started to wheeze its way towards them.

I popped back to my room.

"Good going," Brin said from her place on my bed.

"Are people making weird wishes?" I asked.

She looked blank.

"I heard a woman wish for a cow?" I said. "Someone else wished for a cherry tree. What is up with that?"

Brin laughed. "Sometimes you get the weird ones coming in. They really want something we don't understand. The woman may have been a wannabe farmer, and you could have heard her wishing for a lot of things, all farm-related. She should be thankful she wasn't wishing for fertilizer for her farm. I'd probably have granted it…"

I laughed with Brin.

"Willow?" My mom tapped on the door. Great. I was going to have to explain who I was talking to.

Brin was still giggling but she put a hand over her mouth.

"What?" I called out to my mom. I didn't go to the door.

I was still in pajamas, and my bed was still messed up. It was early for me to be up. Leave it to Mom's radar to be listening the one time I got up early.

I went over to the desk, sat in the chair for a second, and then got up like I was going to the door. I'd pretend I was at the computer and hope she bought that one.

Brin hadn't popped out, so I waited before turning the knob.

"Are you in there with someone?"

"No. I was listening to something on the computer." I opened the door a crack, hoping Brin had had the good sense to move.

"Oh. You sound better."

I shrugged and stared, waiting for her to go.

"Do you want me to make some breakfast? I could do French toast?"

It sounded good. I smiled. "Sure."

She nodded. "About half an hour."

I went back to the computer and sat, just as the wish pressure started to grow again.

"Not again."

"It's been hellish out there. I can feel it when the people I'm watching have to grant wishes. You've had a light morning so far," Brin said.

I glared. I hoped it stayed light, because I hated this. Too much concentrating and looking for safe wishes.

Brin popped out without a good bye, leaving me to listen to the wishes all on my own.

"I wish I didn't have to go to work."

"I wish I had a better job."

"I wish I had gotten the promotion."

"I wish I would get a raise."

It was probably normal that people were wishing about work in the mornings. I felt like I wanted to grant all of them, but I was so busy thinking about the potential downsides, that I wasn't granting anything. The wish pressure grew.

The problem with that though, was that the larger the pressure was, the harder it was to avoid granting a wish when you didn't want to.

I listened some more.

"I wish we didn't have to go to Grandma's."

"I wish I didn't have to go to camp today."

"I wish I could wear my bathing suit all the time."

The mom of that child would no doubt hate the consequences of that particular wish. End dates, kid, end dates.

"Just once, I wish you'd be on time."

Yeah, I popped out for that one. A mom, not unlike mine, yelling at a daughter who wasn't even dressed. They were clearly going somewhere and the girl was dragging. I so felt for her.

But I had to grant a wish and her mom was getting it. Just once right? Worst case, the daughter would be late for everything else, but hey, not my fault. The pink cloud went out and then I was free for a moment.

It didn't last.

Chapter Twenty-One

Some fairy godmothers can arrest the wish granting process if they realize there's a problem — *The Fairy Godmother Handbook*

I had hardly popped back into my room, when the wish pressure started again. Ugh. This was so tiring. I wasn't sure how I was going to get through the day and be able to act human for the interview later on. I changed clothes so I'd be dressed for when I went down for breakfast, which still sounded good. At least I wasn't as bloated as I was yesterday. That was a good thing.

Who knows what my mom would do if I wasn't very hungry again? She'd probably freak out and make me go the naturopath or something. Because you know, anything out of the ordinary is potentially me dying.

The wish words were coming in fast and furious, and I felt myself having to grab at my wish power, even though I really wasn't all that uncomfortable with it. It was like being tired or having granted so many wishes made it harder to hold back.

"I wish I had a decent pair of shoes."

I popped out and saw the wisher, a guy not much older than me, but definitely dressed in worn clothing, shorts and a t-shirt. He also looked like he wanted to go out and run or walk and his shoes were ragged. I let the pink cloud go towards him. His shoes changed while they were on his feet.

He had a pair of red strappy sandals that looked like they were made by Jimmy Choo. Probably not what he was expecting.

I saw him start like he was wondering what the heck happened. Then a look of horror crossed his face as he looked around to see if anyone else was there looking at him. I popped out before I could see more.

Another wish pressure was coming on, but I wanted food.

I went downstairs to where my mother was just starting to put the egg-covered bread into the pan. Maple syrup sat on the table with one plate, just for me. I really ought to get sick more often if she was going to do that.

I got some juice from the refrigerator. It was mostly gone, which meant she'd juiced it yesterday. Hopefully she wouldn't get mad that I drank day-old juice instead of waiting for her to make up something new. My luck, she'd be so worried about my body that she'd juice up veggie juice with no fruit, and I hate that.

Fortunately I had the juice in the glass and the container in the sink, being rinsed before she turned around to see what I was up to. She didn't say anything, although I detected the smallest bit of a frown.

Would it kill her to be too pleased with me?

The wish pressure was getting bigger and I wondered if I should wander off to the bathroom or if I'd be able to eat first. French toast doesn't take long to cook, so pretty soon it was on my plate and I was scarfing it down quickly enough. No bathroom running for me.

I rinsed the plate, working around my mom who was finishing wiping down the counter. When I went upstairs I saw her looking in the fridge like she was deciding what she wanted to juice.

I hurried up before she asked me my opinion, so she could tell me my ideas were bad. Besides, I still had a wish to grant.

Brin was sitting on my bed. "Breakfast smelled good."

"French toast."

"I wish I got some of that."

I let the wish pressure go. Safe enough, right?

"Willow?" my mom called.

"What?" I opened the door a little.

"I had some French toast left over. Why don't you have some more?" She was carrying a plate of the stuff, piled high, probably twice what I ate that morning.

I just looked at her. "I'll see what I can do." I took the plate and closed the door, practically in her face.

Brin started to giggle. I gave her the plate and the fork.

"Don't get crumbs or anything sticky on my bed," I warned.

She dug in, smiling. "No thanks?"

"For what?"

"Helping you with that wish?"

I glared. But it did make me wonder where my mom had suddenly found the extra French toast. Had she turned and it was sitting there on the plate? Did she remember making more? How exactly did a wish like that work?

I didn't have time to think about that too much. The wish pressure was already building up again.

I sighed. I sat down at my computer and listened to all

the wishes, holding onto my power so I wasn't granting everything.

"I wish it was lunch time." Now think of all the things that could go wrong with that kind of wish. I was so not messing with time. It sounded little but the way things were going... nope. Nope. And double nope.

"I wish I had eaten breakfast." Not going to go back and change time, even that little bit. I learned what changing the past could do the hard way, before I learned to control my wish granting power.

"I wish you'd do more around the house!" Clearly a woman yelling at someone. I popped in, thinking I would take a look-see if I wanted to grant that wish. I felt the pink cloud moving out but I grabbed on—I didn't just try and trap it, but I grabbed it like I might grab a rope or maybe a big sheet and I pulled it back.

My feet literally moved across pavement on which I was standing. I was outside a small, older brick house that had seen better days. There was a guy, again about my age, and his mom. She was shaking she was so mad.

"You need to do more around here. I don't care what else you think is so important. So is this house."

He wasn't even watching her. I sort of hated to force a kid into being compulsive about doing "more" around the house. I mean what was "more"? At the same time, I could see he wasn't about to be helpful. She looked tired. Like she'd been working all night and was now home trying to get something done around there. They didn't exactly live in one of the best neighborhoods in Charlotte.

I let go of the pink cloud or rope or whatever and let it flow towards her and her wish. *Bam*. It sort of exploded around her in pink lights. I popped out just as the kid looked up. I thought he saw me, but I couldn't be sure.

I got home and breathed out. Whew. Another wish down.

Another one was building up. This was so not going well.

Brin wasn't in the room, which meant she was either off granting a wish of her own or she was busy watching someone else. I hoped the latter because it meant I wasn't in big trouble. Only minor trouble. I'd take what improvement I could get.

I put on my music to try and do something besides hear wishes, and started playing with my phone. Sage wanted to do something this afternoon.

I told her I had the job interview. Assuming I could still make it with all these wishes building. This was so beyond a pain.

"I wish I had a million bucks." I heard that. Felt the wish power going. I grabbed on, physically and pulled it back into my body. It felt weird, like it didn't quite fit right, like it was folded wrong or something. I was reminded of all the times my mom yelled at me for not folding the fitted sheets right so they weren't flat when they went in the closet.

I listened more carefully. "I wish I could do that kind of thing."

I had no idea what they wanted to do, but I had a sense that it was two people talking and one could do something and the other couldn't. Since when did I know so much about these wish things? Go me.

I popped into a gym to see two women. A skinny woman was telling a fat woman that she wished she could do that. The fat woman was jogging along on the treadmill without a care in the world, while the skinny woman was walking and breathing hard. I totally thought I had things confused but when the wish power went out, it went to the skinny woman.

I popped out about the time another young woman in work-out clothing tried to make eye contact with me. I wondered what she thought.

Back in my room I tried to ignore some more wishes. The power kept coming up. It wasn't bad, like yesterday, except when I waited too long, but it was always there. I was getting tired. I granted wishes for a kid to go out to lunch and get a kid's meal, for a bathing suit to fit a girl when she was afraid it wouldn't, and for an older woman to get a birthday card from her grandson.

I could hardly keep my eyes open. I was getting so sleepy.

"And more powerful," Brin said, popping in. "I can feel your wish granting even when you're not really trying. Impressive."

"Glad you think so. I need a nap."

I fell back across my bed and closed my eyes, hoping to nap. I was about to drift off when the wish pressure pulled me back, much like I pulled the wish pressure back into me.

"I know. It won't let you. I suspect you're tired because you've grown by powers of ten in ability," Brin said. "Lots of seniors aren't able to do that trick of pulling the seed back in once it grows out."

"Can you?" I asked.

Brin nodded.

"Why didn't you tell us about it when you were training us?"

"Not everyone can. You have to have your own picture of how to do it. I see a seed with roots and branches. You see a sort of rope. Everyone sees it differently and works with it differently. I know a woman who pictures herself twining a string of pearls around her finger."

I gave Brin a long look.

"It's not something I can just describe. Even some seniors just can't. Ability and age don't go hand in hand."

"So am I still on the chopping block if I screw up?" I asked.

Brin smiled and shook her head. "Probably not. In fact, I think the full-bloods are impressed with you. If you purposely screw up and do something stupid, you'll be back on the block, but I think so long as you remain sort of aware and don't let your emotions get the better of you, you should be good."

I drew in a breath. Good. Thank heavens. I leaned back on the bed, trying to focus on falling asleep but the wishes were intruding again.

I granted more wishes, noticing as I did that it was almost like skimming through a book, seeing and knowing the information I had at hand. Still, the longer I went, the sleepier I got.

While I was trying to remain in charge, pay attention and not let my emotions get the better of me, I wasn't totally successful. I misheard a wish. Fatigue does that.

Of course I misheard the worst of all possible wishes.

Chapter Twenty-Two

Wishes will be granted via whatever the wish power sees as the path of least resistance — The Fairy Godmother Handbook.

Unless there are sunspots. — Amended by Willow Vaughn.

I apparently listen to kids way too much. I heard this little kid who sounded really excited. I thought he said "I wish I had dessert, sir." Seemed like a safe enough wish. And yes, I know he sounded like he was in a bad English movie rather than a real red-blooded American kid, but who was I to judge? Especially when I was half asleep.

I popped in. I was looking in a big window on a house. The kid was with his father and they were sitting at a dining room table. Okay, so I didn't see plates or anything to indicate they were eating, and I didn't notice anything to do with dessert, but that's why you'd wish for it right?

I let my pink cloud go. And *bam.*

In pops a stegosaurus.

It bashed its tail into a wall, knocking it down, bringing down the main part of the roof.

The last I saw, the kid was smiling and the dad—assuming the guy was the dad—looked kind of horrified.

Shit. I was so in trouble for that.

I popped right back out.

Brin was on my bed again, laying down laughing. "Oh that was rich. Why did you grant a wish for a dinosaur? What were you thinking? Thank god he wasn't thinking of a tyrannosaurus or that other one from the movie, what was it?"

"Velociraptor?" I suggested.

Brin nodded, tears falling from her eyes. Really, she was laughing so hard she was crying. It was so *not* funny.

"I thought he said he wanted 'desert, sir'. Not 'dinosaur'."

That made her laugh even harder. "I can't believe you misheard that. It's not even close!"

"I was practically asleep." In fact, even as upset as I was, I was looking at my bed and wanted nothing more than to roll Brin off of it and just go to sleep. I didn't know how I was going to make it through my interview.

Brin just laughed harder.

"Well, the full-bloods got a kick out of it, although they are annoyed because no one is wishing it away. It's not the worst thing that's happened today at least, so you're safe. And the fact that there are a few of you who are just exhausted and are growing in power works in your favor."

"So what happens now?"

Brin stood up. "Sleep if you can, before another wish comes up and it wakes you."

I was only too happy to oblige. Of course, I dreamed of granting wishes. I kept starting awake, grabbing at something. Brin was there twice and shook her head. The third time, she was gone.

My mom woke me to be sure I got to my interview on

time, which was good, because I was finally asleep without dreaming. There was a slight wish pressure but not like it was earlier.

The outfit I'd put on earlier was all wrinkly, so I put on a different sun dress, but the same sweater and sandals. Hopefully I looked suitable for someone who wanted to be a bag girl. I even pulled my hair back so it looked sleeker. If I was going to have to meet with the store manager, I wanted to look my best.

"Drive safely!" my mother called, humming *A Whole New World*, again. Did she do that to purposely annoy me? It's not like the lyrics running through my head made me think any clearer. I had a moment to consider wishing that she'd never sing that again, but I had to admit, there was that time it might have saved my life, but that's a whole other story.

I got to the grocery store and went to customer service. They had me sit at one of the little tables near the coffee shop, just like last time. The manager wasn't immediately available, so I waited, running my hands along the black top of the little square that they called a table. It would be hard to fit more than a cup of coffee on it if there were two people. Some of the tables had four chairs, and I wasn't quite sure how four people were supposed to fit around the thing at all.

The cash registers were beeping and clicking and drawers were slamming. Underneath that, I heard the radio that always played in the store. It was some oldies station that played kind of lame music, but it wasn't totally horrid. The place smelled of coffee and citrus, and I knew that in the evening it smelled of their freshly-baked French bread, which always made my mouth water. Not that I ever got to eat any of that bread, because my mom hadn't made it herself from her special ingredients.

I shifted a little, looking out the large glass windows. They were tinted, so it wasn't too bright inside, but I'd found a sort of sun puddle where I'd stay warm if the air conditioning got a bit wild—I'd noticed that sometimes that happened in the store. A thin, black woman walked into the store, holding her child's hand. She was smiling, and laughing at something the kid said, and it made me smile too, even though I was tired.

I caught the shine of a red sedan out of the corner of my eye as it turned to park. This was followed by a large gray pillar dropping down onto the ground.

I felt the store move. In fact, the floor tiles under my feet felt like they leaped up. I heard crashes around the store, and a few gasps, but no one screamed, not yet.

I looked out again, squinting, trying to figure out what that pillar was. Everything appeared gray but then my eyes and brain started working together, and I realized the pillar was a leg, and it was attached to the stegosaurus.

Great. I was here at an interview, and the stegosaurus was at the same grocery store. This was *so* not going to go well.

It turned its tiny little head, which was much too small for its large body, and looked at the glass. It opened its mouth like it was going to roar or something, but I didn't hear anything that came out—if it had a voice, it was clearly a quiet one. Maybe it was mad that I had granted the wish that created it.

I had a moment to visualize myself running from the dinosaur, which was chasing me because I'd brought it into existence. I would look so stupid, and I wouldn't get the job at the store—in fact, I'd probably get banned from all the grocery stores, and then I'd never get a car, not that I'd need one, because I'd have been smashed flat by a stegosaurus.

I stood up and backed away from the window. A few other people were crowding in.

"What on earth?" That was an older woman standing behind me. She was pushing a cart of groceries, already bagged.

A tall man in a white starched shirt and black pants with a name tag came up beside her. "I'm not sure anyone should leave right now," he said. He looked over his shoulder. "Have someone stand at the doors and keep people inside. Probably inside the store itself, not the entry."

It sounded like a good idea. The entry he referred to was all glass. It was where they kept the carts and stuff.

"Let's all move out of this area," he said. Then he looked at me, looking me up and down. "Are you Willow Vaughn?"

I nodded, not trusting my voice. I wasn't sure if I'd start laughing hysterically if I tried to talk.

There was a stegosaurus outside the grocery store where I had an interview. That was like totally crazy and funny and sort of scary. What if he stepped on my mom's car? She would be so pissed.

"We'll need to reschedule your interview," he said. "I've got kind of a crisis here."

"I can see that," I managed to say with a perfectly straight face, like this was just another typical store crisis that someone has to deal with every day, because, like, stegosaurus.

"I wanna see the stegosaurus!" This was a dark-haired girl about eight, pulling at her mom, a tiny woman not much taller than her daughter, who looked completely horrified.

Leave it to the kid to recognize a dinosaur. As I moved back into the aisle, wish pressure started to build again. I could have made it through an interview, but I was really worried about what would happen if I popped out now. Would everyone notice?

Okay, yeah, probably not. Everyone was looking at the dinosaur. But what if someone did see me, and connected me to the thing, and then blabbed about it all over? That would be bad.

The dinosaur moved towards the glass and started to knock its head against it. I mean dinosaurs probably hadn't seen much glass in their time, right?

"Let's all move to the back of the store," the manager ordered.

A few people seemed frozen where they stood, staring at the thing. I nudged a few of them along, following behind to make sure they stayed out of the way. This was not altruism on my part. I wanted a front row seat to see what happened.

Of course, when the stegosaurus broke the glass, I realized that may not have been such a good thing. Did stegosauruses eat people?

Chapter Twenty-Three

Don't grant wishes about dinosaurs. It goes really, really badly —
Willow Vaughn

Everyone was in the aisles, separated by cereal and ice cream and mayonnaise, depending upon the aisle they'd chosen to run up getting away from the creature. I was in the aisle of happy little leprechauns and athletes, AKA, the cereal aisle. I suppose that meant I could throw little crispy things at the stegosaurus if he got too close.

Which really made me wonder what would happen if someone pulled out the bug killer from aisle three and started spraying him in the face.

The grocery store no longer smelled like food. It kind of smelled like a bathroom, and I wasn't having to push people along any more either. They were all running for it on their own. I couldn't blame them. I was right behind them. It probably would have been rude to jump over them and hide.

"What is that thing?" Someone screamed.

Now there were screams.

"We shoulda gone for the wine section," I heard a man say, probably one aisle over. "We could have died happy."

I moved towards the back of the store, away from the stegosaurus, but I kept my eyes on him. His head was way small. It seemed like if anyone was going to get killed by that thing it would be because they got crushed under his foot or maybe hit by that tail, which I had only now caught a glimpse of.

There were major spikes back there, and the thing was swinging it lightly, like a cat does before it pounces on a mouse. I wondered if that meant it was mad at us or if it thought we were play toys.

"I shouldn't have come here today," a woman was crying.

"I want to pet the dinosaur!" a little kid cried.

Leave it to kids to not understand that they really ought to be afraid.

I was listening for a wish that I could grant.

Why wasn't anyone wishing this thing away? If I didn't grant wishes, I'd have been wishing that it was gone.

"I wish we were in the wine section," a woman said, probably in response to the man regretting his choice of grocery store aisles in which to die.

The stegosaurus smelled like old musty books that you find in the back corners of used bookstores. Yeah. Mom again. Why buy new when you can buy used?

It flicked its head, knocking over shelving.

We all ran, even me.

Unfortunately I was caught under a falling metal shelf. Cereal boxes crashed down around me, cushioning the blow from the metal shelving. There was even a little space for me to turn over, but my skirt was caught on something leaving me on my hands and knees.

I pulled at it, trying to pull it out but the skirt was

solidly made. My mom always buys the best on those occasions when she buys new. If it had been a cheap dress I'd have probably ripped the seams by now.

Great, I was going to die because my mom didn't like me to buy cheap clothing.

The stegosaurus trudged closer, then sniffed at the boxes. A few had split open on falling and there were flakes and rings of grain scattered around the floor.

The dinosaur sniffed at them again and then flicked out a long purplish tongue as thick as my hand and slurped them up. Then it went around sniffing the floor for more cereal to eat.

I did my best to pull myself away from it and out from under the shelving.

All around me people were screaming.

I heard high pitched screams and groans and moans, or maybe that was me.

Everyone, except the dinosaur, was vacating that aisle.

I was going to get trampled by a wish I granted.

I pulled again, trying to free my skirt, but it wasn't happening.

I could have used a knife but I think those were on aisle four or something like that. I know this place too well. My dad always shops here. They have a decent organic section, not as good as my mom wants, but for last minute pick-ups she'll deal.

I felt something rip a little on my dress. I pushed myself back a little further but then I was hung up again. My skirt hadn't completely ripped free of the shelving.

Something nudged my foot.

I looked back at the dinosaur and its head was under the shelving I was trapped under. Something wet brushed my foot and leg.

I kicked, hitting something that felt like a rock.

The dinosaur tossed its head, throwing the shelving up and off of me.

I scrambled out of there the second I was free.

I plunged into a huddled mass of people, some of whom were climbing over the meat counter and into the butcher's area.

"The door!" the manager was screaming. "Go around to the door! Out the back."

Of course there was only one employee door that I could see, and there was a crowd there, too. It was surprising, because I didn't think the store was that crowded when I came in.

A child was crying, whether in fear or because he wasn't getting to pet the stegosaurus I didn't know.

The shelving crashed back down with a bang and the stegosaurus stepped on it. The metal squealed as the dinosaur pulverized it beneath its heavy gray feet.

Thank heavens I had gotten out of there.

"What is that thing?" someone asked.

"I wish I knew," another person responded. It was an easy wish to grant. The pink cloud swished out of me and over to the man making the wish.

"I wish it were somewhere else," someone else said.

Great. I had missed out on the wish I had needed to make and no one else was listening and helping. Of course, to be fair, it was a pretty vague wish.

"It's a stegosaurus," a man said, it was the same one who had wished to know what it was. "It's a dinosaur of the late Jurassic era which was scattered widely, although most fossils have been found in the western United States and some in Portugal."

At least I wasn't carrying around a wish pressure to slow me down.

Looking at the mess behind me, I had a feeling I wasn't

going to be hearing from this store any time soon. I could see my dream of my own car drifting away from me. Or maybe crushed beneath the feet of a dinosaur that should not even have been there.

The stegosaurus lifted its head like it was watching us.

Then, unexpectedly, it turned to leave. Perhaps it didn't like the smell of meat? It stamped around the store, turning. Then it swung its giant tail.

The air hit my face as it just missed me.

Any shelves still standing were knocked down.

A package of disposable diapers caught on one the dinosaur's tail spikes.

The job of destroying the local grocer done, it stomped out. Everything had taken perhaps ten minutes.

I heard sirens in the distance. The police were here. Like they'd be any help.

Chapter Twenty-Four

Wishes always have consequences — The Fairy Godmother
Handbook

Now that I wasn't staring down a tiny-headed stegosaurus, I could breathe. The floor still bounced when the dinosaur pounded against the pavement outside, but it was much quieter inside the store, or what was left of it.

People were no longer so eager to get out, but there was still a line, because, like, the store was a mess. All the aisles were down except the last row of wine in the wine section. The people who had wanted to be in the wine section may have had the right idea. It seemed to be the only place left standing.

The manager stood shaking his head. Several other people who were dressed in black vests with plain white shirts, were standing around like they weren't sure what to do. The woman from customer service who had helped me earlier was guiding people through the door to the back. I followed slowly behind the mother and child I had seen entering the store.

"That dinosaur was big!" the child said.

You got that right. A good reason not to go wishing for a dinosaur.

I followed them through the back area, where we passed a huge metal walk-in freezer door, all matte silver. The handle was as long as my arm. I felt the chill going past it.

Outside the noise level went up, the heat went up, and the brightness went way up. The air was sort of smoky, sooty and smelled like dust and dirt, which really surprised me because I didn't think dust smelled like anything.

I heard a rhythmic *thwap, thwap, thwap* and I squinted, looking around to see four helicopters circling overhead. Two were close enough that I saw they were the big, black copters that looked like the ones in spy thriller movies. A guy was leaning out of the door, looking away from where we stood.

The earth jumped again whenever the stegosaurus stomped particularly hard. I wondered if it felt good to the dinosaur when it did that.

It was hard to hear anything over the choppers, but I thought I heard several car alarms start to go off. Great. Mom's car was probably smashed, which was going to piss her off.

I tried to think of how to wish away the dinosaur. Wishing it away might just put it somewhere else, destroying another store. I went through a ton of possibilities and all of them seemed risky. To wish it out of existence might mean that dinosaurs had never existed. That one dinosaur might have had a reason for humanity's existence.

Considering sun spots seemed determined to misunderstand wishes, there was no way I was going to make a wish that could do that.

A huge crash sounded, making me cover my ears and duck away. The land seemed to buckle and then it settled again. Dust or smoke rose from my left. I started coughing. Part of the store wall had come down.

The helicopter that had been closest pulled up.

The stegosaurus practically trotted around the side of the building that was still standing. It swished its tail, like it was trying to reach up and hit the helicopter. I wondered if the diaper package that was still stuck on it would cushion a blow.

The dinosaur probably thought the helicopter was the world's biggest fly and was trying to swat it away.

The downside? It was coming right towards us, and things that big cover a lot of ground even when they aren't trying to move all that quickly.

I ran towards the street that wound behind the grocery store. My path took me down a slope and onto a sidewalk.

The stegosaurus was staying close to the building, swatting that tail from side to side.

I watched as it turned to look at the helicopter which was following it.

Then it started running towards us. Maybe it had some sense that there was safety in numbers, even if the rest of us were all much tinier than it was.

Cars had come to a halt on the road, and people were standing outside them looking at the stegosaurus, mouths open.

This was good because the people running towards the street could cut between cars and not get hit by them.

I ran to the side, around the parking lot, out of the direct line of the stegosaurus.

I was still kind of running towards the street so I could

stay ahead of it, but I was working on staying in the parking lot. I needed to see if Mom's car was okay, and I figured if I stayed in the lot when the dinosaur was leaving, I wouldn't have to be chased by it.

This was good, up until the helicopter got in between the dinosaur and the crowd.

The stegosaurus stepped on one parked car and then turned, swishing its tail and sweeping away several others. The crash of them smashing together was loud enough to be heard even over all the other sounds.

Police ran past me.

Someone tried to guide me away, but then they started running.

I looked and yeah, my friend the stegosaurus was running in my direction again.

At least when I saw the tail flail I noticed it no longer had the diapers stuck on it. Now it had a basketball stuck to a different spike.

It was between me and the street so I ran in the opposite direction.

There was a beige and brown Arby's at the far edge of the parking lot.

People were standing outside that building, too, with mouths open. The person at the drive up was leaning way out to look at the dinosaur. This could be bad.

I had a feeling I knew what was going to happen. I tried to think of a good wish. How do you get rid of a dinosaur?

Chapter Twenty-Five

You can't grant your own wish but another godmother may be able to
—The Fairy Godmother Handbook

"I wish this dinosaur would go back to his own time!" I cried. An orange colored cloud surrounded me.

The pounding on the ground stopped. I heard gasps even over the sound of the helicopter. Something stunk. I looked back, knowing there would be no dinosaur. My wish had worked.

What I saw, in the ruins of the parking lot—I mean there were huge pieces of asphalt standing straight up on edge like out of some Hollywood disaster movie—was a large black splotch of some gooey substance. Hopefully it wasn't going to start moving again like some horror movie monster.

Mom tells me I have a wild imagination.

"Is that tar?" The man behind me muttered.

Wrinkling my nose I identified the stink. Yep. Tar. Ugh.

People were walking around, looking at the parking lot. Those who had run into the street were looking around as if trying to see where the stegosaurus had gone. I could only imagine what they were all thinking.

I looked over to where I'd parked my mom's car. I couldn't see it, but all the cars over there were pretty messed up. I walked slowly in that direction.

The police were all walking towards the tar splotch. They were being very cautious. One even had his hand on his gun. Like a hand gun would have stopped that thing? Did he get a look at how thick its skin was? Not that I had been poking holes in it or anything, but the skin seemed to be the consistency of an elephant's.

I passed by a white Toyota lying on its side. A little ways away a blue Honda was smashed flat. Next to it was an equally pancaked Ford truck and a black Dodge Ram. I guess if a dinosaur steps on you it doesn't matter how tough you are.

It didn't look like anyone was in the cars, thank heavens. Mom's gray Prius was standing on one end leaning against an overturned Subaru. The front end looked pretty smashed up.

This was not going to be a fun phone call, but better to get it over with. I pulled out my cell phone.

"Mom?" I said when she answered.

"What's wrong?"

"Have you seen the news?" I asked.

"What's happened? You weren't taken hostage or something?"

"Um no?" What was up with the hostage thing? Like did that happen? Here in Charlotte? At a grocery store?

I wasn't quite sure how to tell her that a stegosaurus had rampaged through the grocery store, and I'd nearly been killed and her car was damaged. I wondered if insurance covered loss by dinosaur. I giggled.

"You sound funny. I'd come pick you up but you have the car."

"And that's the thing," I said. "There was this big thing, like a dinosaur, in the parking lot of the store, and well, the car is smashed up against a Subaru."

"Willow Vaugh!" she exclaimed. Then her voice got very low and very shaky. "Are you taking drugs?"

I rolled my eyes. "No." I put as much no power into that as I could. "I was at a job interview, remember? Even if I did want to take drugs I would *so* not be taking them then. And I think I won't be getting a job here any time soon."

"What did you do?" Yeah because it had to be my fault.

"I'm going to start walking home," I said. "But you and dad will have to come back here to look at the car. Maybe by tonight it will have cleared out and you can see it."

"What do you mean cleared out?"

"There are helicopters circling, and the police, and there are a lot of damaged cars and people parked on the side of the road who were looking at the creature." I was crossing the street towards my subdivision. A few other people were wandering away too. I heard a few people swearing, no doubt over damaged cars.

The Mazerati symbol I nearly stepped on didn't bode well for that car.

"Willow…"

"Maybe just turn on the news," I said.

I hung up, sighing.

It was hot.

Too bad I couldn't stop into the store for some water. I

considered begging some from the fast food place, but they appeared to be closing up. There was a gas station two blocks up. With any luck they were still open and not too busy.

Chapter Twenty-Six

Some wishes just aren't going to turn out well no matter what — The wisdom of Willow Vaughn

My feet were sore and I was exhausted by the time I got home. I had already needed more sleep when I went out to the store. I had probably survived only because I was too scared to fall asleep. Walking home had worked off that rush.

My mom was sitting slack-jawed in front of the television when I got home. I looked over her shoulder and saw someone had a jerky camera shot of the stegosaurus. The basketball was on its tail, so it was right before it disappeared.

I wondered what happened to the basketball back in the Jurassic period. I giggled, thinking about a scientist finding that thing fossilized with the dinosaur.

I went upstairs and fell into bed, not caring what I looked like. Sometime later my mom woke me up for some soup and made me change clothes.

She was surprisingly good about not annoying me with

questions. Of course, it was dark by then, and that meant my dad was home, so I probably had him to thank for that reprieve.

I ate, explaining what I had seen. I was too tired to make anything up or to offer any explanations for why it had happened. My folks seemed content to discuss the theories offered on television. I ate my nice, safe, homey, chicken noodle soup with Mom's homemade bone broth from real, pastured, all organic chickens.

The television was still on, and I listened to a familiar voice talking about dinosaurs on the news. I looked up and saw the man from the grocery store. "I just knew what it was, but the dinosaurs were wiped out millions of years ago. I have no idea why—or how—one of them would have just turned up like that," he said.

"Do you suppose this was a prank? Maybe for a new movie?" the reporter asked.

"You weren't here," the man said. "There was no way this was a prank. The stegosaurus was perfectly formed, down to the last plate that stood on its back. It was a quiet thing, making nearly no noise, but when it moved, the earth trembled. No one could fake that. It destroyed the store, and ran around the parking lot, smashing up cars, Then, it just disappeared."

I went back upstairs, considered a shower, decided it was too much work and fell back into bed and slept.

Brin was waiting when I woke up. There was a faint wish pressure, but it was after eight, and that was the first time I'd woken up at all. The sun was coming through the blinds, just enough to tell me that it was a whole new day.

"That was some afternoon," Brin said.

"I can't believe that my wish worked," I said. "What was up with the tar?"

"I guess dinosaurs become oil and this was oil," Brin

said. "Believe me, it was far from the worst thing that happened yesterday."

"What else?"

"Look it up," she said, pacing over to the window. She opened the blinds and looked out, letting in way too much light. I didn't say anything as I sat down at my computer to see what else had happened.

A small hill in California had erupted volcanic ash, and now there was a huge cloud all over the place. Scientists were looking into it. In Greenland, a large hunk of land had cleaved off and was floating in the ocean, its own island, not part of a glacier. Again, scientists were looking into it. It appeared that that part of the country was pretty uninhabited, although a few people who had been out hiking had to be rescued.

A kid had grown an extra head. Three Russian girls were now boys. Just like that. Their families were appalled. The girls weren't sure what to think. My impression was that there was more to that story than anyone said.

A dolphin had to be rescued from a rooftop in Miami, which was no small feat. It involved a helicopter ride to a facility that had enough water to be sure it would live. There were reports of a yeti wandering around Disneyworld but there hadn't been any confirmation of that report. People claimed a dinosaur had gone on a rampage in Charlotte. Scientists, of course, were investigating.

I smelled bacon from the kitchen. I decided I should get dressed and go eat breakfast.

Brin smirked. "Be careful with your wish-granting today. It should be better but you never know."

She popped out before I could say anything.

I changed while I had privacy, or as much privacy as I was going to get. I mean, was she secretly watching me or something? How much did she know about my life when she had to 'keep an eye on me'?

I went down to the kitchen. Mom had made a frittata. She was also cooking up some bacon in the frying pan. There were plates in the sink, so my dad had had some earlier and probably Eric.

"Eric was up early again," I said, taking a piece of the frittata.

"He's got to work," my mom said. "I'm still not sure about you looking for a job. Are you sure you want to work in a grocery store?"

I crunched on a piece of bacon and when I'd swallowed, I answered. "Dad and I talked about it. I'll probably get paid better there than if I do something in retail." Although it would be fun to work in a clothing store. I heard there were discounts.

Mom frowned a little and nodded.

I was feeling quite a bit of wish pressure by the time I finished my breakfast. Apparently I wasn't going to get out of granting any wishes today. But at least they weren't coming so fast. Mom put all the pans away, leaving me to wash my plate, which I did. I even put it in the dishwasher, which had a few other things from breakfast, none of which looked completely clean.

I went up to my room and started leafing through the wishes I heard.

"I wish I could find my purse." I granted that without even popping over. I mean how bad could that be? I knocked on the wood of my headboard after thinking that.

I waited in my room, listening to music, wondering if I'd have to grant another wish. By lunchtime I was feeling like today wasn't going to be nearly as bad as Wednesday, which was a huge relief.

Friday was much the same. I granted a wish for a

teenager to find his missing cellphone. I popped out for that one. I was standing in the shadow of the upraised asphalt in the grocery store parking lot. The store had police tape all around it and boards over the windows. Men in hardhats were looking things over. Several carried clipboards. I thought I saw the manager with them but I couldn't be sure at that distance.

The teenager was a young guy, about my age. His head was shaved flat. His face was smooth mocha and he looked near tears, searching for the phone. He was walking around the parking lot that still had some overturned cars, but most were gone. I knew ours was gone. Mom had called the insurance agent yesterday and they had taken care of it.

I let my pink cloud go. I felt good, like I'd done something someone wanted, but I also felt bad because I knew this wasn't going to end well. And it didn't. His cell phone was smashed. I popped out as he started swearing.

On Saturday I didn't have to grant any wishes, but on Sunday I had two wishes to grant, both small things.

The first was for an older man wishing his son would come home safely. I felt good about that one.

The second wish happened about an hour after that one. It was a woman who wished she didn't have to trim her toenails so often. I wasn't sure about that one, but I didn't feel badly after granting it. I hoped her toenails didn't fall off.

Brin didn't pop in once and I was grateful. Things were slowly getting to be more normal again.

Chapter Twenty-Seven

Granting a useful wish makes the granter feel good. — The Fairy Godmother Handbook

I woke up Monday with another bit of wish pressure. I knew that the sun spots should be going away, so maybe this would be my last wish for a while. I wondered what we'd talk about at the meeting tonight.

The pressure built up hard and fast. I wasn't even really up, still in my pajamas, when I had to start searching for a wish to grant. It was like having to go to the bathroom really bad and dancing around until you got there, except this was searching through wishes.

"I wish it hadn't happened." No.

"I wish he'd care." Better, but still no.

"I wish she were cleaner." No.

"I wish she didn't make that sound." Um no. Might be someone breathing.

"I wish she'd be quiet." Really no.

Come on.

"I wish I'd won." Changing the past, no.

"I wish I could run like that."

Pop. Ready to grant a wish. Looking at a seven year-old kid in a wheel chair. Did I do it? The wish was already starting to flow out. I tried to pull it back. Maybe too big of a wish? Could it go badly?

But it was a strong wish pressure and it slipped through my fingers, though I grabbed at it and tried my best to pull it back. I'd done it last week, darn it. I had to admit, though, that I was just pulling because I was afraid of what could happen with that wish, even though I kind of wanted that kid to be able to run like he wanted. Which was maybe why I couldn't grab onto the wish and stop it. At any rate it slipped through my fingers.

The pink cloud went off towards the boy in the wheel chair. He was in his home, watching television some guy running in an old movie, probably a chase scene. I looked closer, and man the runner resembled the guy who had wanted to purchase a house, except, considering this movie was in black and white and the guy buying a home was only in his twenties, probably, it couldn't be. Could it?

I saw the kid kind of itch at his legs, like he was wondering what was going on. I popped out before I saw anything more.

Brin wasn't waiting, so apparently letting a kid run when he hadn't been able to before wasn't going to get me in major trouble. Minor trouble, maybe. But I could handle that. I mean, I'd almost gotten kicked off the wish-granting team, or whatever it was, and had nearly died by dinosaur trampling. Minor trouble was nothing.

Other than that wish, which did stress me a bit, because it was a bigger wish than I'd granted for the several days, nothing else happened. I did mess around on the computer for a while, looking to see if there were stories about the kid. I had no doubt there would be if I kept searching.

I did see a story on a dance troop that had all broken their legs doing a new move. All sixteen of them. I had to wonder if that was a wish gone bad. I kept searching for anything on the boy.

An hour later, I realized I had spent an entire hour wondering how a wish could have gone wrong. I'd never have done that two weeks ago. I mean I hadn't felt bad about letting the wish happen, but then again I hadn't felt bad about granting a kid a wish about a dinosaur either. Normally when a wish is bad, you feel sort of bad. When a wish is good, you feel good. And I had felt good.

In fact, it was only in the last couple of days that I'd started feeling good about wishes again. Maybe this whole sun spot thing was fading.

"Willow?" my mom said as she knocked on my door.

I opened it.

"Call Yvonne," she said. Yvonne was a friend of hers from the Farmer's Market. She had a shop there called Soap and Goats. Basically, she made homemade all organic soaps and also spun yarn from goats she raised on a little farm a few miles outside of the city. That farm was the site of one of the most boring afternoons ever when my mom took me to watch her shear the goats.

"Why?"

"She had a job opening and I told her you were look- ing. She wants to see if you're interested."

"It's not, like, shearing goats is it?" I asked. I mean I knew that Yvonne's business had gotten big enough that she had her cousin spinning yarn, too, so she would have time to keep making soaps.

My mom laughed. "No. She just wants someone to do some packaging for mailing out orders. She can't handle it all any longer. She'll pay more than minimum wage, and you'll get more useful skills than you will if you work at a dress store. She'll want you to input data on what you're doing and things like that, too."

I took the note and gave my mom a long look. I was so hoping this would work, I was almost tempted to wish as I dialed my phone.

Chapter Twenty-Eight

Active sunspot times are great times for training new fairy godmothers
—The Fairy Godmother Handbook.

Um. No.
— Willow Vaughn.

The Monday meeting was quieter than it had been the week before. Brin showed up late.

"Sorry." She waved a hand. She was dressed sort of like a 1980s Madonna, from the black dress and off-center hair bow to the fingerless gloves.

"Any news?" Grace asked from her chair. We'd compared notes on what had happened with our various wishes. Paula had had a bunch of lions show up in a town, because someone wished all the *lying* would be displayed in the town square.

Sergei had accidentally granted a wish for someone to be loved by everyone. The woman was still fending off suitors.

Grace had granted a wish for someone to get the most

prolific knitter award, which seemed safe enough, but they now had a compulsion to knit that wouldn't go away.

Deliza granted someone's wish for a fur coat. They now had to get shaved daily. Deliza giggled as she said it, a surprisingly young girlish sound. I laughed too because it made me think about the old woman I had turned into Wookie Woman.

Sue, who almost never talked, said she granted a wish for someone to see an eagle, which had then appeared in their living room.

Cole shook his head. He'd granted the guy a wish for stronger eyesight. Whenever he looked at someone they fell over. The guy found that wearing sunglasses helped.

The icebergs that had been melting had gone back to how they were at the turn of the century, then promptly began to melt again, causing flooding thanks to Connie. Three buildings had disappeared because feral cats didn't like them. Also Connie. Because Connie could speak to cats and grant their wishes. Yeah, I know. Don't say it.

"It seems like things are starting to go back to normal now," Brin said. "But you still have to be careful with how you grant wishes. Double-check all your instincts."

Brian started to say something. Grace started to add a "But…"

Brin held up a hand. "I know. It's hard. Just be as mindful as you can. Do your meditation and whatever else you can to make sure you aren't just expecting a wish to be granted. Watch what you hear. Lions and dinosaurs aren't normal wishes."

"It's not fair," I said.

Brin glared at me.

"I thought I heard *dessert sir* and got *dinosaur*. Paula did hear *lying* but she got *lions*."

Brin shrugged. "It's almost like the sun spots liked

playing games isn't it?" She had kind of a funky smile on her face that made me suspicious.

"Is that what was going on?" Jesus asked. He clearly noticed the smile, too.

"I have heard rumors that the sun spots interfere in ways that make it appear so. The magic seed isn't completely without sentience. I'm sure as things go wrong, it can enjoy having fun."

"You said it had been like nine hundred years since the last time this happened?" I clarified, hoping it would be that long again before it happened. If I was still a godmother then, and that was a big if, at least I'd be a senior and probably have more control. Although Brin had said I'd already gotten better control.

"Since the last one. They think it will be about fifty more before the configuration happens again. I guess we're heading into an active time. But you'll still need to take care this week and try and not just grant the first wish you focus on…"

"That's just not possible!" Grace said. She said it with such force she practically stood up. Really.

"Willow can do it," Brin said. "I saw her. So did the full-bloods. That means they'll expect that your group will learn a little something and at least some of you will try to not grant the first wish you focus on."

Everyone, and I mean everyone, turned to look at me.

"But she granted a dinosaur!" Paula protested.

"And the never dying." Sue added.

Yeah. Remind me of all my failings.

"That's right," Brin smiled again. "But she also learned how to *not* do that. So she can teach you."

"What?" That was a general chorus, including me. I am so not a teacher. Besides, I was just a kid, and these were adults.

"You heard me. Willow figured out how to hold onto wishes. While not everyone can do it, I want her to teach everyone how to try."

Grace glared at me. I had a feeling that of all of us, Grace was the oldest, not only in terms of looking her age, but in how long she'd been a godmother. She wasn't exactly pleased that I was now considered an expert on something. In fact, no one looked particularly pleased, although Paula and Connie didn't seem to have any particular problems with the concept.

Brin finished her part of the meeting. I tried to offer my perspective on holding onto a wish.

"It's like a big rope or something and I grabbed onto it and pulled it back to me," I said.

Everyone looked dubious. "Try grabbing on to something next time you have to grant a wish."

Still dubious stares.

I tried explaining it a few other ways but no one was really getting it. I suggested they think about a rope they could use to pull the wish power back in like, they were hauling in a fish. A couple of folks nodded at that.

I sighed. It would have to be enough. Everyone else clearly thought so, too, because Connie suggested that it was getting late and we should be leaving. I was only too happy to pop out. I was actually disappointed not to see Brin in my room. I really needed to give her a piece of my mind about this teaching thing.

Epilogue

Senior fairy godmothers have been granting wishes for at least 500 years.
— *The Fairy Godmother Handbook*

The next week I granted more wishes, but they were all normal wishes, and I was starting to get a sense of whether they were good or bad. You know, like someone wanting to not be sick actually got well, and I felt good about it. It was what usually happened when I would grant a good wish.

I didn't grant anything really bad, although there was a woman who wished the air conditioner didn't blow right over desk, and the whole darn thing stopped working. I heard about that one, because it was a hot week and all the employees in that building were sent home. I hadn't felt really bad about that wish, so I guess it was okay that the air conditioning broke.

As for the kid who wanted to run, there was finally an article about him. He'd just gotten up out of his chair one day after his legs started itching, and suddenly he could walk. He was walking a lot now, from what I heard. That made me feel good. Of all the wishes I'd granted in the last two weeks, at least one had worked out.

My mom's car was totaled, and she and my dad had to get a different one. She was not pleased about that. The good news was that she wasn't exactly blaming me for it, and the insurance had paid, even though no one could explain exactly how the car had gotten smashed.

Yvonne hired me to do her mailing and packaging. She was teaching me how to wrap up the soaps and pack things in boxes. She was a little bit of a perfectionist about how things should be packed, but at least I could wear shorts, and I had really flexible hours, so it wouldn't interfere when I went back to school.

Yvonne planned a few minutes at the end of each week to work out a schedule for my hours the following week. I always got to sit with her and agree to them or not. So far it wasn't bad, but, I mean, it's not like I wanted to pack boxes all my life.

At any rate, I was still granting wishes so apparently I was still a fairy godmother, which had had me worried there.

By the end of July, I was halfway to my goal of saving up for a car, which was going to be so cool. Sage and I were talking about what kind I should get. I wanted a cute little sports car, but there was no way my dad would say yes to that. Sage thought a Jeep Wrangler would be cool, because you could take it anywhere.

I wasn't sure I wanted something that big, so I'd probably be looking at a used hybrid, like a Prius, which was sure to make my folks happy. Or maybe a Fit or a hybrid Civic. My mom had suggested both of those. I guess she doesn't want me to have the same car as she does.

But at least those were normal teenage worries. Which meant my life was back to normal.

Except for the fact that, yes, I am a teenaged fairy godmother and I grant wishes. But at least now I wasn't fighting sun spots, too.

About Bonnie Elizabeth General

Bonnie Elizabeth has been writing since she was eight years old when she wrote her first book on several pieces of lined paper. The manuscript has long since been lost.

Since that time she has worked at a variety of jobs including veterinary receptionist, cemetery administrator and licensed acupuncturist. She has continued to write in a variety of venues, from blogging to writing about acupuncture under her full name and title, Bonnie Koenig, LAc.

Bonnie writes the popular Whisper series of novels as well as writing a variety of short fiction. You can find her books and stories at all your favorite ebook retailers.

Don't forget to look for One Bad Wish, the first Willow Vaughn book!

Stay in Touch